"You're mad. You don't wager homes. Wives. Families. You can't take someone's wife."

"You can if she's wagered."

Sam swayed on the arm of the sofa, swayed and laughed. She had to laugh. She didn't know what else to do. This was absurd. This was a farce. It had to be. Johann was trying to scare her, trying to make a point. "Exactly how much do we owe you?"

Cristiano stood. Broad-shouldered and powerfully built, he wore his dark hair long, so that it brushed the collar of his coat. "Nothing now, Baroness van Bergen, your husband has managed to settle his debt."

Jane Porter

TAKEN BY THE HIGHEST BIDDER

FOR Love OR MONEY

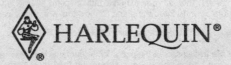
HARLEQUIN®

TORONTO • NEW YORK • LONDON
AMSTERDAM • PARIS • SYDNEY • HAMBURG
STOCKHOLM • ATHENS • TOKYO • MILAN • MADRID
PRAGUE • WARSAW • BUDAPEST • AUCKLAND

ISBN 0-373-12508-9

TAKEN BY THE HIGHEST BIDDER

First North American Publication 2005.

www.eHarlequin.com

Printed in U.S.A.

CHAPTER ONE

SAMANTHA VAN BERGEN'S husband was missing in action. Again. And unfortunately, Sam knew where he was.

She knew where to find him when he didn't return home for days at a time, and she knew what to expect.

Disaster.

This was a battle, she thought, drawing her gray velvet cloak closer to her evening gown as she swiftly climbed the stairs to Monte Carlo's grand Le Casino, a battle she was losing.

Johann had always been a compulsive gambler but he used to win more. He used to walk away from the table when it turned ugly. But he didn't do that anymore. He just sat there, losing. Losing. Losing.

They'd already lost so much. Their savings. The chic penthouse. The Ferrari—not that Sam had ever driven it.

What was left? She wondered, climbing the casino's marble steps.

In Le Casino's VIP card room, Cristiano Bartolo lounged at his favorite table when the door to their private room opened. Annoyed by the interruption, he glanced up, but his irritation eased as he recognized beautiful, blond Samantha van Bergen, or more commonly known as the baroness van Bergen.

It was, he thought, mouth curving faintly, such a huge, stately title for such a young blushing English bride.

He played his card, then looked up to watch her unfasten the top hook on her velvet cloak, letting the dove-gray velvet fabric fall back over one shoulder revealing her white evening gown beneath.

She fascinated him. He didn't know why. He'd only seen her once before, but she'd made such an impression that night six months ago he knew he'd never forget her.

The first time he'd seen her had been here, at Le Casino, as well. Then, as now, he'd been sitting at the exclusive high roller tables, and then, as now, every head at the table had turned. Cristiano turned, too, to see what had caught every man's attention.

No wonder every man stared.

The baroness was small, slim, beautiful. She had a delicate oval face framed by blond ringlets, long loose curls that gave her a decidedly angelic appearance, although her eyes, slightly tilted at the corners, were not completely innocent.

Beautiful girls were a dime a dozen, but she touched him; with her serious expression, her dark brown brows pulled, the deep furrow between arched brows.

Cristiano watched now as the young baroness stood just inside the door, not nervous or uncertain, just focused. She wore a look of utter concentration, an expression of grave concern, and Cristiano was certain this is what Joan of Arc must have looked like before battle as she moved to Johann van Bergen's side.

Cristiano had never liked Johann, would never like Johann, and had deliberately sat at this table so he could play the baron. Cristiano had discovered months ago that Johann van Bergen didn't know how to play cards, couldn't gamble and hadn't a clue how to walk away from a game even when he was being bled. And he was most definitely bleeding tonight.

Bleeding out.

Bleeding dry.

Cristiano scooped up a handful of chips, moved them forward, upping the ante by two hundred and fifty thousand pounds. It wasn't a small bet, but neither was it huge. Over five million pounds had already been wagered tonight. Johann's loss to Cristiano's gain.

Eyes narrowing, Cristiano watched as Samantha approached

the table, watched one long loose blond tendril slide forward on her shoulder, dangle across her breast. He envied the curl. Longed to take it, twine it around his fingers and then dip it between her full breasts.

Cristiano reached for his whiskey, sipped it, let the heat and fire warm him, wanting Samantha. She made him feel—curious, carnal, intent on possession.

She crouched now at Johann's side, her velvet cloak pushed back on her shoulders, her slim bare arms extended, her hands on Johann's thigh.

Her hands didn't belong on Johann's thigh.

Her hands belonged on his.

Cristiano's gaze moved from her bare arms to her shoulders to her deep cleavage revealed by the plunging neckline of her white evening gown. Leisurely he let his gaze travel up, along the smooth column of her throat to her firm rounded chin and jaw, the curve of cheekbone and the worry in her blue eyes. The worry was also there in the faint line between her perfect arched brows, as well as in the press of her lipsticked mouth, her beauty delicate and yet painfully pinched.

Angels shouldn't be so tormented, he thought, finding his chair suddenly uncomfortable, just as his body felt too hard and tight.

He imagined kissing her full mouth until it softened beneath his, saw her lying naked in his bed, her slender limbs stretched out beneath him, her delicate gold necklace the only thing she wore.

But his blond Joan of Arc was on a mission, and she was oblivious to all but Johann as she spoke to him, her voice but a murmur of soft sound. Cristiano couldn't hear what she said to Johann van Bergen, but the baron made no effort to lower his voice. "Go," Johann told her, tone cold, blunt. "Go back home where you're supposed to be."

But she didn't go. She continued to crouch at Johann's side, whispering urgent words only the baron could hear, words that only angered him further. "I don't need a mother," he said, slapping his cards down. "I already had one. And I don't need you. You've done nothing for me."

Two dark pink blotches stained her cheeks. Silently she regarded him, face flushed, chin lifted, painful dignity. Then without another word, she slipped off her cloak, handed it to the gentleman at the door and took a chair, sitting behind Johann.

During the next hour and a half Cristiano watched her. He liked watching her. She'd been beautiful six months ago but she was even more stunning tonight. He'd have her. Soon. Very soon. Even if she was another man's wife.

Cristiano folded his cards, tossed them onto the table and leaned back, content to use the time to watch his woman. Because she was his. She was everything he wanted—young, sleek, sexy and unavailable. The unavailable aspect he found especially seductive.

It was good to feel tempted. Seduced. It felt good to want something, *someone*. It made him feel, period, and God knows, he didn't feel much of anything anymore.

Lashes lowered, he watched Baroness van Bergen now as again she whispered more urgent words to her husband. But her husband was ignoring her.

Foolish man, Cristiano thought derisively. Foolish man to marry such a woman and then ignore her. Because there was beauty, and then there was beauty, and Johann's young blond wife wasn't your run-of-the-mill beauty, but something finer. Rarer.

Cristiano called Johann's bluff, forcing the baron to show his cards. Nothing.

It was all Cristiano could do to hide his contempt. Johann was gambling his life away. What a fool. A gambling man understood risks, and took them. A gambling man understood wins and losses. But Johann wasn't a true gambler, he didn't understand risk, and he didn't understand loss.

But Cristiano did. He knew what it was to win, and he knew what it was to lose and he didn't like losing. So he didn't. Not anymore. Hadn't lost in so long that he'd almost, almost, forgotten the bitter taste.

Almost.

But not quite.

And that faint but bitter taste of loss still burned his tongue as it burned his heart and made him take. Risk. And win.

It was conquering. It was plundering. It was—he reached for the cards just dealt him—revenge.

Sam sat behind Johann, her gaze fixed on his new hand of cards, seeing what he was seeing, wondering if he was as nervous as she. He had terrible cards. Absolutely nothing in his hand and yet he was sitting there playing as if he held only aces in his hand.

God, Johann, what are you doing?

What are you thinking? Playing?

Stomach in knots, hands folded on her knee, Sam drew a deep breath, her white jersey dress with the gold spaghetti straps pulling tightly across her shoulders.

The villa was gone.

The bank account emptied.

There was nothing left to wager.

With a cry of disgust, Johann tossed his cards onto the table, showing what he had. Nothing. Three sevens.

Sam bit the inside of her cheek to hide her shame. Three sevens. He'd bet and lost their home with his three sevens. God forgive him. Where was his common sense? His survival instinct? What kind of fool was he?

"I'm out," he said, sitting back, running his hand across his darkly tanned face. Johann, an Austrian baron, playboy and fixture on the Monte Carlo scene, diligently maintained his deep tan by sunbathing daily on the pool terrace, usually with a stiff cocktail at his side. "I've nothing else, Bartolo."

Thank God, Sam thought, eyes burning, body alternately hot and cold. He was done. It was over. Let them go home now and figure out what they were going to do. "Johann—"

"Be quiet," he snapped.

She flushed, bit her tongue, knowing the man called Bartolo watched and listened to everything. She knew Bartolo had watched her tonight, too, had felt his gaze rest on her repeatedly, and each of his inspections grew longer, heavier, more personal until she thought she'd scream for relief. He made her feel strange.

He made her feel alone. And hopelessly vulnerable.

It wasn't a way she wanted to feel. Not now, not ever.

But now Bartolo smiled lazily as he lay down his own cards. "You were on a winning streak for a while."

"I nearly had you," Johann agreed, signaling for another round of drinks.

Sam's hands tightened on her knee, convulsively squeezing her kneecap. *No more liquor,* she prayed, *no more liquor tonight. Let's just go, Johann. Let's leave here…*

"So close," Bartolo said.

Sam hated Bartolo then, realizing for the first time that he had been expertly baiting Johann tonight, egging him on. But for what purpose? He'd already stripped Johann of everything— house, wealth, respect. What else was there to take?

Johann nodded. "So close." He paused, studied the other man. "One more hand?" he proposed, taking the bait.

The air bottled inside Sam's chest and her nails dug into her hands. Damn Bartolo, and damn Johann. Johann couldn't be serious. He couldn't possibly think he'd win, not playing Bartolo, and certainly not after drinking. *"Johann."*

"Shut up," Johann said without looking at her.

She flushed with fresh shame but she wasn't going to shut up, wasn't going to let this slaughter continue. Bartolo was amoral. But she knew what was right, and this wasn't right. "Come home with me now, Johann. *Please.*"

"I told you to shut up," Johann snapped.

The heat scorched her face. It was humiliating being here, humiliating running after a man, begging a man to stop, think, pay attention. But she'd do what she had to do. She'd do anything for little Gabriela.

"Johann," she pleaded softly.

Johann ignored her. But Bartolo looked at her, a long measured look that went straight through her. A look that said he was merciless and proud, hard and unforgiving. Ruthless. Savage. Bloodthirsty.

She leaned forward, touched Johann's shoulder. "Johann, I beg you—"

Johann reached up, shoved her hand off. "Go home before I ask that hotel security walk you out."

"You can't continue," she whispered, face, body, skin aflame. She was mortified, and terrified. The future had never seemed as dark as it did that moment.

Johann looked up, nodded at the plain suited security guard standing just inside the VIP room's door. "Could you please see the baroness out?" he asked, even as he took the fresh cocktail from the waitress. "She is ready to go home."

All eyes but Johann's were on her but she didn't move, didn't even flinch despite the plainclothes security guard at her elbow. "This isn't right," she said out loud.

But no one answered her and she felt Bartolo's eyes. His gaze burned, seared. Punished.

The guard bent his head, murmured, "Madame, please."

Madame, please leave without making a scene. Madame, go home while your husband loses everything and everyone.

Furiously, reluctantly, Sam stood, her gown's white jersey fabric falling in long elegant folds. "If you can't think of me, Johann, can you please think of Gabby?"

He didn't answer her. He didn't look as if he'd heard her. Instead he was drinking hard, throwing back his cocktail even as the dealer was dealing a new hand.

Escorted by hotel security, Sam walked silently through the casino overwhelmed by the clink and bells and whistles of the one-arm bandits edging the casino floor. She hated casinos, hated the noise, the garish colors and lights, the artificial glamour that seduced so many.

Fortunately the security didn't touch her, push her or rush her. There was no hurry. She, like the hotel staff, knew what happened now was beyond her control. No one would stop a gambler, not even a compulsive gambler. Monte Carlo had been built on the backs of those with deep pockets and a dearth of self-restraint.

Back at the small town villa in the historic district, Sam collected a sleeping Gabby from the neighbor's house, carried her home, put her in her bed and after a lingering glance into the little girl's simple bedroom, shut the door.

Sam curled in a chair downstairs in the living room, a blanket pulled over her shoulders. The house was chilly but Sam couldn't turn up the heat. There wasn't money to pay for such extravagances. There wasn't money for anything.

Tears started to her eyes but she pressed a hand to her face, held the tears back. Don't cry. You can't cry. Tears are for children.

But some tears fell anyway, escaping from behind her hand, from beneath the tightly closed eyelids.

It was all too bitter, too brutal, too lonely. She'd tried so hard to give Gabriela a better life. That's why she'd married Johann, that's why she put up with his abuse. Sam had done everything in her power to help things here, improve things for the child. But none of it mattered. Johann was determined to gamble and drink, no matter the cost.

Much later she finally fell asleep, still huddled in the armchair and didn't wake until she heard Gabriela bounding down the stairs.

"Where's Papa?" Gabby asked, nearly five years old and endlessly enthusiastic.

Gabby had already dressed in her school uniform and even in her dark gray uniform with the white piping, Gabby was beautiful. A day rarely passed without someone stopping Sam to comment on Gabriela's stunning looks, and Gabby was stunning.

Gabby's mother had been a model from Madrid. She'd done some small films in Spain and hoped to go to Hollywood to try her luck there, but died tragically a year after Gabby was born. The details about Gabby's mother's death were all a bit sketchy, but Gabby had inherited her mother's Spanish beauty with her classic features, her dark hair, and those green-gold eyes bordered by shamefully long, jet-black lashes.

"Good girl, you're all ready," Sam said standing and folding the blanket. "And your papa's out but he'll be back later," she added, trying to look unconcerned, trying to look as if she hadn't spent the night crying in a threadbare overstuffed armchair worried sick about a future that looked increasingly bleak and chaotic.

"He hasn't been home in days," Gabby complained. "And you're still wearing your fancy dress."

It was Sam's one and only fancy dress. Sam checked her smile, knowing it was brittle, and false. "I fell asleep reading," Sam fibbed, refusing to worry Gabby. "But let's have breakfast now and then we'll do your hair for school."

Sam kept Gabriela chattering until she'd walked her to school a quarter mile away, but once Gabby ran into the building, leaving Sam on the pavement, Sam felt her defenses crack and fall.

What *were* they going to do? How were they going to manage? No home, no money, no food, no tuition for Gabby's school…

Sam had nothing of her own, not even a bank account. When Johann married her, he stopped paying her a salary and what little Sam had saved over her years as a nanny had been spent on Gabriela. Johann had never understood that little girls quickly outgrew their clothes and even much beloved dolls eventually wore out.

As she walked the eight large city blocks back to their villa town house, Sam struggled with the reality of their lives. In the four years she'd been with the van Bergens, things had gone from bad to worse, and worse to nightmarish. If she had family, she'd take Gabby and go there now. But Sam had no family, had spent most of her childhood and teenage years in the orphanage in Chester.

She'd left school at seventeen, and with the help of a parish scholarship, attended Princess Christian College in Manchester, but even with the scholarship she'd had to work several jobs to pay her bills.

Money had always been very tight. Sam had never been spoiled. And yet even living frugally, and even knowing how to scrimp and save, Sam knew her situation now was far more dire than it had ever been. Sam knew she could fend for herself. But what about Gabby? How would Sam take care of Gabby if they had no home, no income, no place to go?

Climbing the four steps of the town villa, Sam entered through the front door and was just about to unbutton her coat when she heard Johann call to her.

"If you could spare a moment, Baroness. I'd like to speak to you."

If *she* could spare a moment? Oh, that was rich, Sam thought, following the sound of Johann's voice to the living room.

Late-morning light flooded the windows, patterning the wood parquet floor in great sheets of light, the usual blare of horns and noise from Monte Carlo's busy streets failed to penetrate the walls and windows of the old villa. The room, she thought numbly, was quiet. Too quiet.

She faced him, hands bunched inside her coat pockets. "Yes?"

"Do take off your coat," he said irritably. "You make me nervous standing there all bundled up like that."

Silently she unbuttoned the tweed coat, tugging it off her shoulders before laying it across the couch. "What did you want to speak to me about?"

Johann clasped a drink in his hands, the glass resting on his chest. "I've settled my debt to Bartolo."

The dark gloom hanging over her head immediately lifted. Sam felt almost dizzy with relief. She couldn't hide her smile of delight. "You did? Excellent! I'm so glad—"

"He'll be here in an hour to collect you."

It was too rapid a mood swing, too harshly said. Sam exhaled hard, then breathed in again. *"What?"*

But Johann didn't speak. Instead a deathly quiet shrouded the living room. Sam held her breath, not thinking, not understanding, certain Johann would clear the misunderstanding.

Yet he said nothing.

She heard nothing.

Only the clink of ice shifting and melting in his glass.

"Say something," she choked, feeling as if she were suffocating in the heavy stillness.

"I did. You just didn't like what I said."

Little spots danced before her eyes. This couldn't be happening. She'd heard wrong. Had to have heard wrong. "Then say it again."

Baron van Bergen's lashes dropped. "You heard me the first time."

Sam couldn't believe it had come to this. He'd been an addict ever since she'd met him but this…this…

This was unthinkable.

Impossible.

The end of reason itself.

Sam took a frightened step toward him before freezing, unable to take another. "You *didn't* give me away."

Johann's eyes opened briefly, and he shot her a dirty look before slinking lower in his chair and keeping his cocktail tumbler pressed to his forehead, expression increasingly pained.

"I didn't *give* you," he contradicted sourly, eyes closed. "I lost you."

"*Lost* me." Her voice nearly broke, her English accent sharper, more pronounced. Sam balled her hand in a fist behind her back, nails biting into her palm. "How could you *lose* me?"

"Things happen."

He was wrong about that, Sam thought, hands tingling, body cold and icy as if her blood had frozen in her veins. Things only happened to Johann van Bergen. "To you," she said bitterly.

He opened one eye, looked at her, deep wrinkles fanning from his eyes. "Since you're not doing anything, *liebchen,* could you get me another drink?"

Liebchen. Liebling. Nothing like good old German endearments he didn't mean, had never meant. Seething, Sam dug her nails harder into her skin. *"No."*

Grunting, Johann rolled the cold tumbler across his forehead.

He was obviously hungover. He'd been out all night, had only recently stumbled in. "Explain this to me."

His lashes lifted, his pale blue gaze slid over her, inspecting her. "Is that a new dress?"

Sam glanced down at her cream brocade dress with rich lavender and purple threads, the hem of the dress edged with silky purple ribbon. The dress had been part of her trousseau two years ago, part of the elegant designer wardrobe Johann had bought for her before she'd discovered he was deep in debt and couldn't afford groceries much less fine clothes. "No. We can't afford new clothes, remember?"

He grunted again, rolled the glass in the opposite direction over his brow. "*Mein Gott,* you remind me of my mother. She was a nag, too."

Sam didn't flinch, stooping instead to numbly pick up a gold tasseled pillow that had fallen from the threadbare sofa onto the hardwood floor and tossed it back onto the couch.

Johann could mock her all he wanted. Theirs had been a marriage of convenience. Nothing more, nothing less. She didn't care now what he thought of her, hadn't cared for his opinion when she'd married him. The only reason she'd agreed to the marriage in the first place was to protect his child. A child he seemed determined to neglect and reject.

"I'm not going to him," she said now, "Or with him, or anywhere near him. You'll have to find another way to settle your debt."

"Oh, you're tough now, are you? I wonder if you'd be so tough if I'd wagered my darling daughter instead of you." He paused. "Gabriela, my beautiful little angel daughter." He laughed low, mockingly and shook his glass, rattling the ice cubes. "I did consider it, though. More than once. But Bartolo was interested in you. Not sure why. You've no money, no education, no connections, no family. You're British. Boring. And might I add, frigid."

"It shouldn't matter if I'm frigid since there won't be any physical intimacy."

"Not with me, anyway. But I can't see him taking you and not taking you, if you get my meaning."

She did, all too well, and it was all she could do to keep her disgust from showing.

To think that Johann would wager her…

And to think that this Bartolo would accept…

Sam had put up with Johann's abuse for years and she told herself not to let the insults hurt, told herself his opinion didn't matter but on the inside she was cold, so cold, as if the December chill had burrowed all the way through her. She was there to protect Gabby, nothing else mattered. "So what happens now?"

"Cristiano comes to get you. You're his problem now and I wish him all the luck in the world."

"Johann!"

"Must you talk so loud? I've a hellish headache."

She lowered her voice marginally. "This isn't funny."

He slunk lower in his chair. "No, it's not funny. I've lost everything. My cars. My penthouse. Now my villa. It's all gone."

Her throat felt raw. She couldn't disguise her bitterness. "Why do you gamble?"

"Christ, Sam, it wasn't like I killed someone." He took a gulp from his glass. "It was a mistake."

Sam stared at the man who'd been her husband for exactly four hundred and sixty-five days and her employer for two years before that. He was an alcoholic, a gambler, a womanizer and the father of the most amazing, beautiful, and once lonely little girl in the world. "What happens to Gabby?"

"I don't know. She never came up."

"Well, I won't leave her here with you. If I go, I take Gabby with me."

Johann took another great gulp, draining his glass. "I don't think that's up to you. It's not up to me anymore. It's his decision. He's the one that owns you."

Owns you. Owns. Like meat. Or a piece of property. Real estate in the Côte d'Azur. Eyes burning, her throat swollen, Sam swallowed the pain. Intellectually she knew Johann had never loved her, never wanted her, had only married her to keep Gabby's mother's family from taking her, but still, his coldness, his indifference and cruelty cut.

"You'll use Gabby to force me into another man's bed?" Sam sank down onto the edge of the couch.

"Well, you were no use in mine."

Sam felt a moment of panic, pure unadulterated panic. At twenty-eight, she knew who she was, and what she was, and Johann was right. She wasn't a sexual woman, not even a sensual woman. Despite the wedding ring on her finger, she had no knowledge of men, of sex, or desire. And she was content to leave it that way. A woman didn't have to be sexual. A woman didn't need a man. She'd been alone for years but she wasn't alone anymore. She had Gabby. She loved Gabby. "I'll do this…go to him…settle your debt, on one condition. You let me adopt her."

"It's out of my hands."

He acted as if Gabby was nothing more than a tennis ball. He'd just throw her in any direction, toss her where it suited him. "Impossible! You're her father, her legal guardian—"

"But I told you, Sam. God, I do wish you'd listen." Irritably Johann pressed the crystal tumbler to his temple. "Cristiano is coming for you. He wants *you*. *You*. Understand?"

She heard him, but she didn't understand.

The idea of a man wanting her was more than she could comprehend and she stared at Johann so long it hurt her eyes, her mind, her heart.

Baron van Bergen was handsome and dissolute. Selfish. Impulsive. Immature. And the father of the most gorgeous child with the most beautiful heart. Sam had been a nanny for some of the wealthiest, famous families in the world and she'd never met a child like Gabriela van Bergen before.

"I want to see him," she choked. "I want to see him now."

"He's coming later, Sam."

"I won't wait. I must see him now. I must speak to him now—"

"And tell me what?" The voice drawled from the doorway and even without looking Sam recognized the voice. Cristiano Bartolo. The devil had arrived.

CHAPTER TWO

AN ICY heat washed through Sam. Skin prickling, she turned on the sofa's arm to face the door and was immediately struck by heat, a dark heat that seared and burned from all the way across the room. "How did you get in?" she demanded.

Cristiano held up a key ring. "My key."

"Your key."

His broad shoulders twisted and he smiled that same mocking smile he'd smiled last night. "My villa."

It wasn't much of a villa, not in its current state of shabby disrepair. When Sam first met Johann, he had a larger, finer villa on the Rock, close to the royal palace, tucked in an elegant old square, set off by equally elegant old fountains, but as his financial picture changed, so did their accommodations.

"You're mad," she said, digging her hands into the couch, looking at Johann, heart racing, adrenaline surging through her in sickening fashion. "You're both mad. You don't wager homes. Wives. Families." But Johann's eyes were closed, his empty glass cock-eyed in his lap and Sam's glance swung wildly back to Bartolo. "You can't take someone's wife."

"You can if she's wagered."

Sam swayed on the arm of the sofa, swayed and laughed. She had to laugh. She didn't know what else to do. This was absurd. This was a farce. It had to be. Johann was trying to scare her, trying to make a point. Obviously he was in over his head.

Obviously he'd lost a great deal of money last night. "Exactly how much do we owe you?"

The man stood several inches taller than Johann, but was twice as thick through his shoulders and chest. Broad shouldered and powerfully built, he wore his dark hair long so that it brushed the collar of his black leather coat. "Nothing now, Baroness van Bergen. Your husband has settled his debt."

She ignored the dart of pain inside her chest. Johann had settled the debt by giving her away. She knew her husband didn't love her, or like her, but still, to be traded, bartered, it was so brutal it wounded. "I'm obviously not for sale, Mr. Bartolo. It's a mistake—"

"No mistake," he interrupted almost gently. "We've met with lawyers, signed papers, sorted things legally. I've absolved him of his debt. Therefore, you leave with me."

"Leave with you," she repeated dumbly.

"Yes. You might be married to Johann, but you're not his woman anymore. You're mine."

Anything she was about to say slipped from her lips. How to answer that bold, arrogant, appalling assertion?

Silent, she looked up at him, and what she saw filled her with fresh fear.

He was calm. Relaxed. Completely in control.

She struggled to match his calm. "Mr. Bartolo, if you'll tell me what we owe you, we can get this sorted out." She tried to look him square in the eye, wanting to demonstrate her strength, but it meant tilting her head back and now, with her neck exposed, she felt even more vulnerable than before.

"You think?"

Sam didn't like looking up at him, didn't like the expression on his face, in his eyes. He was like a wolf alone with a penned lamb.

But she wasn't a lamb. And she wasn't an ingenue, either. She'd lived for twenty-eight years, had been a nanny for nearly ten. She carried no false illusions about life. Or men. Perhaps there were a few good ones, but most were very selfish and none were saints. "What do we owe you?" she repeated crisply.

"This isn't about money, Baroness."

"It's always about money, Mr. Bartolo."

Deep grooves bracketed his mouth. His eyes, neither green nor gold, warmed. "You don't think it could be about love?"

She tried to laugh but it came out broken, strangled. She'd been in love once, years ago, and it had ended so swiftly, so tragically she knew she'd never love again. "You don't even know me, Mr. Bartolo."

"I know what I see."

"Hair? Eyes? Face?" She snorted contemptuously. "That's not love. That's…" And her voice faded as his gaze met hers and she saw in his eyes something so intense, so explosive…fear lapped at her, hot, dangerous, deadly.

His eyes never left hers. "What, Baroness?"

Her limbs went weak, so weak it was as if she were swimming in cold, dense, murky water. Her head spun. Her legs felt close to collapse. "Indecent," she whispered, the only word coming to mind. And it was indecent. His thoughts. His actions. His words.

"And maybe it is." Still smiling faintly, he glanced at his watch, then shook down his sleeve. "It's nine now. I'll send my car for you at four. That should give you enough time to pack, say your goodbyes and do whatever it is you need to do."

She looked away, vision blurred, mind equally fogged. Sam had nothing to pack but it was the goodbyes that tore at her, the goodbyes she feared most. She loved Gabriela as if the child were her own. "You really intend to do this?"

"Baroness, your husband owes me over ten million pounds. What do you expect me to do?"

The faint, hysteria-tinged laughter was back. She felt her eyes burn, her throat seal closed. She turned to Johann who was slumped in his chair, eyes closed, jaw slack, oblivious to the world. "Forgive and forget?" she suggested huskily, hopefully.

Cristiano made a short sound, rough, impatient and yet his half smile hinted at amusement. "You don't know who I am, do you?"

"Should I?" Even as she asked the question, she searched her memory, seeking some clue to his identity but his name still meant nothing to her.

Although she'd lived in Monaco for nearly four years, she'd paid scant attention to the principality's golden crowd. Having nannied in the past ten years for some of the most wealthy and famous people in the world, she was neither impressed nor influenced by those with money and fame. In her experience, the rich were rude, and the famous forgettable.

"No. The only thing you need to know is that I'm not a good loser." His hazel-green gaze fringed by jet-black lashes met hers and held. His gaze was steady, too steady. "I hate losing. So I don't."

He walked out then, heading straight for the front door, and for a moment Sam remained where she was, frozen on the arm of the sofa like one of La Palme d'Or's ice sculptures.

Then the ice shattered as she thought of leaving Gabby, saying goodbye to Gabby, and grabbing her coat, Sam raced out of the house down to the front where Cristiano was climbing into a low red Italia Motors sports car.

She reached the side of his car, opened the passenger door and leaned in. "You can't do this. I can't do this. I've Gabby—"

"She's not your daughter."

Sam looked at him where he sat in the driver's seat, dark hair rakish, deep hazel eyes intense and she shook her head, denying his words, denying what they represented, when she knew the truth. Gabby was her daughter, the daughter of her heart anyway. "I won't leave her."

"Baroness, I have places to be, a meeting at the Hotel de Paris in ten minutes—"

"Then give me those ten minutes." Sam pulled on her coat. "Take me with you and talk to me while you drive."

"I won't have time to bring you back."

"Fine." She climbed into the passenger seat, closed the door. "I'll walk back. I don't mind walking. But we must talk about Gabriela. It's important."

Cristiano shot her a long, hard look before starting the car and pulling away from the curb. "Talk," he said as he swiftly merged with traffic. "You've ten minutes."

Sam bunched her hands in her lap, watching Monaco's picturesque streets flash by. Her heart was pounding and her hands were shaking and she had to draw a deep breath to steady her nerves. Thank God Gabby was still in school for the rest of the morning. Maybe, just maybe, this nightmare could be fixed before Gabby returned at three.

But before she had a chance to talk about Gabby, Cristiano's phone rang and after checking the number, he took the call. It was a relatively long call and he was still on the phone when he slowed in the driveway approaching the Hotel de Paris. Tourists filled the elegant square, spilling from tour buses and vans onto the different plazas, snapping photos, posing for pictures, clustering outside the historic Café Divan inspecting the menu.

Sam took in and dismissed the throngs. Monaco was always crowded. Daily tourists, from all over the world, overran the tiny principality eager to visit the fabled home of Prince Rainer and his late wife, the former American film star, Grace Kelly.

What she wanted, needed, was Cristiano's attention. What she wanted, needed, wasn't going to happen.

As valet attendants came forward to take the car, Sam fought tears. He hadn't even given her the time of day.

Stepping from the car, Sam smoothed her coat over her dress and waited in front of the Hotel de Paris while Cristiano finished the call.

Anger burned in her, anger and indignation. What kind of man took a woman from her family? What kind of man would accept a wagered wife?

It disgusted her, horrified her, and her hands clenched helplessly inside her coat pockets, her gaze fixed on the hotel's belle epoch architecture. Be calm, she told herself, be calm. Losing control won't help anything.

She focused on the hotel's architecture instead. The Hotel de Paris and Le Casino were both constructed in the middle of the nineteenth century on a square overlooking the sea. She'd read somewhere that the square had once been an untidy wasteland, overgrown with dense vegetation, hiding deep in the cliffs near seawater-filled caves.

Apparently the famous Monte Carlo Le Casino had been built first, and the hotel second, the hotel just steps from the casino. Once the hotel was finished, stables were added to house horses and carriages, then a fountain designed, and finally gardens landscaped with imported palm trees to create an exotic tableau to lure winter weary Parisians.

Sam was no Parisian, but she was weary. Very weary.

He had to let her explain about Gabby, had to listen to Gabriela's situation. Gabby couldn't be left with Johann. Johann might be her father but he wasn't to be trusted, especially not with a vulnerable child.

Abruptly Cristiano finished his call and put away his phone. "I'm sorry—"

"No. *No,*" she said fiercely, hands bunching into fists inside her coat pockets. "I won't go."

"Baroness—"

"You don't understand. This isn't about me, it's about Gabriela."

His hard expression briefly eased. "I'm not sending you on your way, Baroness."

"You're not?"

"No. I was going to say, I'm sorry I had to take the call, but I've taken care of my meeting. There's nowhere I have to be for the next hour. We're free now to sit down and discuss Gabriela."

Sam felt relief and embarrassment wash through her. "I'm sorry. I didn't realize. I thought…assumed…you were giving me the brush-off."

His eyes, hazel green and gold, warmed. "Give you the brush-off? Baroness, I've just spent ten million pounds to make you mine. The last thing I want to do is give you the brush-off."

His. There was that possession again. His, to be his, to belong to someone. To belong to a man.

It was odd, she thought, nerves twitching, her body so tense she felt like the tightened strings on a violin, but she'd been married twice and had never belonged to a man. And now Cristiano Bartolo talked about possession and yet there'd be no marriage.

Life was strange. No, make that impossible.

"Shall we go in?" Cristiano said, gesturing to the hotel.

"Mr. Bartolo?"

"Yes, Baroness?"

Something in his voice made her blush, and she took a step back, her skin tingling, a fire burning from the inside out. He was hard, male, confident. Strong.

Very, very strong.

And that's what unnerved her most. Sam wasn't used to male strength, hadn't experience with a man like Cristiano Bartolo. Yes, she'd been married twice, but neither husband had been strong, or male, like this. Neither husband commanded attention, seized control, shaped the world to suit them. "I haven't agreed to anything," she said breathlessly, "you do realize that, don't you? I'm here to talk—that's it."

The corner of his mouth lifted in a faint, mocking smile. "You do know the moment a woman throws up walls and restrictions, a man's determined to destroy them?"

The tops of her cheekbones burned. Even her ears felt hot. "I'm not trying to be provocative."

"But that's the charm, Baroness. You're provocative just by being you." And turning, he climbed the hotel's marble steps giving Sam no choice but to follow.

Sam noticed how the doorman jumped to attention, and while he nodded politely at both, he murmured a warm welcome to Cristiano.

Sam glanced back at the doorman as they entered the hotel's grand domed lobby. "He addressed you by name," she said.

"I'm a fixture here."

"You have quite a few meetings here, then?"

"If you want to call them meetings."

A cryptic answer, but one she understood perfectly well.

Maybe she hadn't had sex, but she knew what it was. "So you meet women here?"

"I have a room here."

"Always?"

"When I feel the need to entertain."

When he wanted to sleep with a woman. She turned away, stared across the lobby feeling ridiculously old and prudish. She'd never thought she'd end up twenty-eight and celibate. When Charles proposed, she'd thought she'd have such a different life. She'd be a wife, lover and mother. Instead fate intervened and she'd become this. Tired. Worried. Worn.

"I can show you my suite, if you'd like," he offered.

They were standing in the hotel's grand lobby now, almost directly beneath the vast blue glass dome and Sam flashed him a look of disdain. "No, thank you."

Cristiano laughed, softly, seductively. He liked that flash of fire in her. It was a relief to know she wasn't always so grave and serious. And yet already the spark in her was gone, replaced by more quiet worry, the line of which was almost permanently etched between her fine brown eyebrows.

Last night she'd looked regal, a conquering warrior, and yet today in the morning light, dressed in her simple, sturdy tweed coat, her fair English complexion tinged pink and her blue eyes wide, round, he thought she looked very young, very English, and very scared.

Cristiano liked women, enjoyed women, but he didn't enjoy them scared.

He wanted Samantha, wanted to own her, possess her, but not trembling like a frightened puppy in his bed. He wanted a woman, a strong woman, with spirit.

"Well, you will see it," he said lazily, "the question is just—how soon?"

Sam was listening to him, she was, and yet his words didn't penetrate her brain.

Instead she watched his mouth move, the lips parting, shaping, and she found herself fascinated by the shape of his mouth, the hard lines of his face. He had a strong jaw, strong straight nose, fiercely black eyebrows and then there was that cleft in his square chin and two deep grooves on either side of his firm mouth. His eyes, thickly lashed, were neither green nor gold, but hazel, what ought to be an ordinary hazel but there was so much heat in his eyes, so much spirit and intelligence his eyes fairly snapped with energy. With life.

Again it struck her that he was awake. Alert.

Alive.

Had she been with Johann so long she'd forgotten what it was like to speak to a man that really looked at her? Listened to her? Had she been so isolated these past four years she'd forgotten how men behaved?

"How soon until you see it, Baroness?"

Samantha blinked, knew she'd missed whatever question or point Cristiano had just said. "I don't know," she stammered.

He inclined his head, then turned, and walked through the hotel's grand lobby toward one of the sitting areas at the far end of the room.

Sam had to hurry to catch up with him as he walked. He was tall, broad shouldered, and his steps, long but measured.

"We must talk," she said breathlessly, trying to keep up with him.

Cristiano barely turned his head to look at her. "About what?"

She nearly sputtered in surprise. "You know perfectly well what I've come to discuss. It's barbaric. Inhumane. You don't gamble with people's lives, much less children's lives."

He slowed his pace as they reached the low velvet couches upholstered in royal shades of purple, red and blue. "I don't gamble with lives. I prefer cash. Stocks. Real estate. Unfortunately your husband had just you left so he offered you up."

"You didn't have to be unscrupulous, Mr. Bartolo! You could have taken the higher, moral ground."

Cristiano's eyebrows lifted, one black eyebrow arching slightly higher than the other, and Sam thought he looked exactly the way the devil would, if the devil played cards. "And why would I want to do that, Baroness?"

Samantha's breath caught in her throat as she stared into

Cristiano's face. He was tall, big, broad. *Taut*. He'd walked with a long even step, his arms loose at his sides, apparently at ease, but she was far from relaxed. His very ease unnerved her. "Because you're a gentleman, Mr. Bartolo."

The corner of his mouth curved, a brief mocking smile. "You shouldn't make assumptions. They're usually wrong."

Then he sat down, a slow drop into the low upholstered sofa. Sam remained where she stood, her mouth open with disbelief. He was mad, she thought, nearly as mad as Johann. "And what about Gabriela? What about *her?*"

He shrugged, stretched a long arm out over the back of the sofa. "What about her?"

"She can't be left with Johann. He's not a fit parent."

"Then surely she has another relative who could take her, someone better suited to parenting a young child?"

"She might, but I don't know of anyone. I think her mother's family wanted her once, there was going to be a custody trial, but that was years ago. I don't even know where to find her mother's family now."

He studied her for a long moment, hazel gaze assessing. "Why didn't her mother's family win the custody battle?"

Sam swallowed, plagued by guilt even two and a half years later. "I married Johann. To give Gabby—and prove to the court that she had—a stable, loving family."

"Even though you knew it was a lie?"

Sam ducked her head, didn't answer. She knotted and unknotted her fingers before finally sitting down in a chair opposite him. "I did it for Gabby, to protect her. The court did award us custody, and Gabby trusts me, Mr. Bartolo. She depends on me. I can't let her down."

"She's not even your daughter and yet you're so very protective of her."

"I have to be. Someone has to be."

Cristiano's eyes narrowed as he studied her tight expression. "You love her."

Without a doubt. "Yes."

"And your husband. Do you love him this much, too?"

Sam's eyes closed and she sagged inwardly, exhausted, overwhelmed. She'd never loved Johann even though she'd tried initially. She'd thought maybe her kindness, her compassion might save him…that her love could maybe make them a family but she'd been wrong. Naïve.

Opening her eyes, the fatigue weighed even more heavily on her. She felt as if she'd been battling to save Johann for far too many years now. She didn't know how to keep fighting for him, for the family, for security any longer. The task had become too great, the toll too much. Living with Johann had drained her. "I've done my best to protect him."

"And is that the same thing as love?"

Her lips curved grimly. "It is what it is, Mr. Bartolo."

Cristiano's expression didn't change, and yet Sam felt something shift—her? Him?—and when he spoke again, the mood somehow was different. "I don't like your husband," he said. "I have never liked your husband, but I like him even less now."

"Because he wagered me?"

"And then tried to sell his child, the very child he refused to give to her family."

Her mouth went dry and she felt like a marionette doll, odd, gangly, all wooden arms and legs. "He wouldn't sell Gabby."

"He tried. It wasn't enough he'd settled his debts with you. He thought perhaps he'd buy back some of his lost property, an even exchange, the town villa for his daughter."

"*No.*"

"Yes, indeed."

Sam looked past Cristiano to the creamy marble columns supporting the ornate stained-glass dome. "And what did you say?" she whispered, her mouth so dry, her throat scratchy.

"I don't buy children, Baroness."

She shook her head, shocked. She knew Johann was selfish and a drunkard, a gambler, and a player—but this…it was repulsive. "Do you see why I can't leave her there? Do you see why I must protect her?"

"Baroness, I have no authority over her. I can't take her. Only the courts—"

"But I can!" Sam clasped her hands together, leaned towards Cristiano, hands pressed as if in prayer. "I'm still her step-mother."

"Johann won't allow it. Not if he thinks he can get me to pay for her."

"How much?" Sam whispered. "How much does he want?"

"Three million. The price of his town villa."

Her eyes burned and she smiled bitterly to hide her pain. "I was ten million and his child was only three?"

"My thoughts exactly."

Sam ground her teeth together, panic growing on the inside. Panic at the future, the present, panic that she was losing her grip on reality, panic that it seemed she was going to lose Gabby.

"Sit back," Cristiano said. "Breathe. You look as if you're going to faint."

She shook her head, woozy and nauseous all over again, and struggled to speak, but couldn't find her voice, couldn't even shape her lips. Her face felt stiff, frozen. Her whole body trembled.

Cristiano reached out, touched her arm. "Do you need water?"

She shook her head again. "No," she croaked, but she did feel terrible. Terrible, horrible, devastated. It was as if her world had been a little snow globe and it had been dropped, shattered.

For a moment Sam did nothing but concentrate on breathing, in and out she breathed, deep slow breaths to ease the pain inside her. But just breathing didn't help. If she breathed in, it hurt. If she exhaled, it hurt. Nothing would change the pain.

"She's not your child," Cristiano said quietly.

Anger rolled through Sam, hot and wild, cutting through her fog. "But she *feels* like my child, and I'll protect her like my child, and I will worry about her, and I will worry for her. You can be selfish and cold but I won't be."

"No, I know you won't be. That's why I wanted you. That's why I played hard for you. You didn't fall into my hands by chance."

If he hoped to reassure her, he was failing, miserably. Every word he spoke only heightened her unease and the sense that everything was changing—quickly, dramatically, drastically—and Samantha resisted change, particularly if it was beyond her control. "You wanted this?"

"Very much so."

"You can't take another man's wife."

One of his strong black eyebrows lifted quizzically. "You do if she's neglected."

Dazed, she gave her head a slight shake and Cristiano merely smiled, a cool smile, much like the glittering light thrown off by the huge chandeliers overhead. Neither his smile nor the bright light above them warmed his eyes now.

"Doesn't it grate you, Baroness," he said after a slight pause, "that while you've scraped and struggled to pay bills, your husband sat in the casinos for months losing thousands a night?"

It did, oh God it did, but she couldn't find the words, or the protests. She blinked, held back the tears. "He stopped for a while."

"Not very long. I know. Because every time he lost, I won. And everything he offered, I took."

"So this is your fault."

"He's a compulsive gambler."

"It's a *sickness*."

"So I discovered."

"And could you show no mercy?"

"No." And his expression slowly changed, jaw firming, cheekbones jutting beneath hard eyes. "I am not a merciful man."

CHAPTER THREE

CRISTIANO SENT SAM home in a taxi and traveling back home, she glanced at her watch constantly. Two minutes later, five minutes, eight.

She felt obsessed with time. Driven by time. It was a quarter to noon now. Cristiano had said the car for her would arrive at four, which meant she now had less than four hours to pack and arrange her life, less than four hours to say her goodbyes. Which really meant saying goodbye to Gabby. Four hours to say goodbye after four years of being together…

Sam couldn't fathom it, couldn't get her head around it. The situation boggled her mind, not because Johann had gambled and lost his entire fortune, but the fact that she'd been dragged into this. Johann and Cristiano's gambling had nothing to do with her, or Gabriela. If they wanted to gamble, let them live with the consequences. She and Gabriela shouldn't have to suffer for their poor decisions.

And Gabriela would suffer if Sam left her. Gabby wasn't even five, and yet how many homes had she known? How many different guardians and adults had drifted in and out of her life? How many had actually helped her? Considered her needs before their own? How many had given *love?*

Love, Sam silently repeated, stepping from the taxi, there was a concept. But it was love Gabby needed, not things. Love, not money. Love, not power or control or whatever it was men seemed to think made the world go round.

And facing the tired villa in need of repairs and refurbishment, Sam knew what she needed to do. She needed to take Gabriela away from here, far from the brittle glamour of Monte Carlo, the selfish, greedy games Johann and Cristiano had played, the shallowness of people who cared more for money than a child. She'd been pushed too far this time.

Johann was wrong and so was Cristiano. Sam refused to let Gabby be hurt yet again. Once Sam knew what she needed to do, she also knew where she'd go. The moment Gabby came home from school they'd be gone.

Upstairs, Sam checked the bedrooms and discovering Johann still passed out facedown on his bed, she quickly packed, knowing they didn't need much for their trip—clothes, yes, and Gabby's favorite toys but there weren't many toys, there hadn't been money for toys in the past year.

Quietly Sam opened the drawers in Gabriela's dresser, scooped up the small shirts and skirts, tucking them into the smaller of the two suitcases Sam had brought with her from her last job in Seattle.

Then Sam went to her room—she and Johann had never shared a bedroom—and packed her own suitcase. It would be cold in England this time of year, far colder than it was in Monaco and the south of France, but it would be safe. Cristiano wouldn't know to look for them there.

Suitcases packed, Sam double-checked that she'd put all her documents in her purse, their passports and the other things she'd need once they reached England, then called a taxi.

Inside the door to Gabriela's bedroom, Sam paused, glanced one last time around the room that had been a nursery when Sam had arrived three and a half years ago.

The room was still pale green and white, a scheme that should have been garden fresh but just looked severe thanks to Johann selling the carpet, furniture and artwork out from beneath everyone's feet whenever money grew tight. And with Johann's gambling problem money always grew tight.

But now Johann and his problems would soon be behind

them. In less than an hour she and Gabby would be on their way to a new life far from Johann's drinking, indifference and abuse.

By the time Sam had finished packing, it was time to meet Gabby. On her way out the front door, Sam set their two suitcases just inside the door, ready to be carried to the taxi the moment it arrived.

Sam spotted Gabby as the little girl skipped down the school's front steps and Sam lifted a hand in a wave. Gabby waved back eagerly. Bless the child. What a love she was. In all her years Sam had never met anyone—child or adult—so ready to love, and be loved. Gabby's heart was pure gold.

Gabby burst through the school gate, threw herself at Sam's knees.

"How was your day, my pet?" Sam asked, hugging her.

"Very good. But I forgot I had sharing today. I didn't take anything." Gabby's eyes, a lovely green-gold, darkened briefly with emotion before brightening. "But then Mademoiselle said we could tell a story, and I told a very funny story about a mouse that lived in Daddy's pocket and the adventures the mouse has at Le Casino."

Sam blanched, set Gabby on her feet. "You told a story about your papa at the casino?"

"No, Sam, not *Papa,* but the *mouse* in Papa's pocket."

"And did the mouse stay in your papa's pocket?"

"No. He played cards with Papa at the casino. But he was a very clever little mouse and he didn't lose. Not like Papa. And everyone wanted the mouse because the mouse won so much money he bought us a big new house and a car just for you and me so we could go driving whenever we want." Gabby took a breath and beamed up at Sam. "Isn't that a good story?"

Sam felt sick inside. "You are a very clever girl, Gabriela Grace, but you know that, don't you?"

Gabby just laughed, and they walked hand in hand back to the villa, but the closer they came to the villa, the more Sam worried. How was she going to break the news to Gabby that they were leaving? How was she going to tell her they were going to live apart from Johann in a country Gabby had never even been to?

Oh God, none of this was easy.

And reaching the old town villa not far from the Place de Casino, it only got harder, as parked in front of the villa was Cristiano's red sports car.

Cristiano, dressed in the same black slacks and thin cashmere sweater he'd worn earlier, appeared as they entered the house. "Good afternoon, Baroness."

Gabby looked at him, not at all shy. "Who are you?"

Sam struggled to think of an answer and it was Cristiano who smoothly replied, "A friend of the family's." He extended his hand to Gabriela. "I'm Cristiano Bartolo. What's your name?"

"Gabriela Grace van Bergen."

"A big name," he said dryly.

"I'm a big girl," she answered smartly.

Cristiano's smile turned wry. "Out of the mouth of babes." He turned to Sam. "I see you've packed."

Again her heart sank. "Yes, but I—"

"Is Papa here?" Gabby interrupted, tugging on Sam's hand.

"He's upstairs sleeping," she answered woodenly, as Gabby dropped her hand and charged up the stairs. How could Cristiano persist with this? Maybe he wasn't a gentleman, and maybe he wasn't merciful, but cruel?

With Gabby gone, Sam took a step toward Cristiano, dropping her voice. "You can't do this to her. Please think it through, please try to see it from her perspective. I'm the closest thing to a mother she knows."

Suddenly Gabby was running down the stairs again, her long dark braids flying. "Sam, Sam! Papa's gone. He's not in his room. He's not even here."

Sam wasn't sure if she felt fear or relief. Unbuttoning her coat she faced the stairs where Gabby was charging down. "Maybe he went for a walk."

"No, Sam, he's *gone*. His clothes, his coat, everything's gone." Gabby jumped down the last three steps, going forward to her knees before catching herself with her hands. She righted herself, stood. "He must have gone on a trip without us."

Relief, fear, hope, panic—they pummeled Sam one by one. If Johann was gone, then Sam couldn't leave Gabby behind. But if Johann was gone, and Cristiano didn't want Gabby, then Gabby would be placed in government care until Johann was found.

Stricken, Sam looked up, straight into Cristiano's face. This was *his* fault, Cristiano Bartolo's fault. He was the devil himself, smiling, playing cards, buying drinks for Johann. Sam knew he'd deliberately gotten Johann drunk, too, upped the stakes, challenged Johann, pushing him out of his comfort zone until Johann was playing over his head.

But then, Johann always played over his head.

Sam couldn't look away from Cristiano's hard impassive features. He looked perfectly neutral, even indifferent. And she may have disliked him before, but she hated him now. Hated his confidence, his arrogance, the power he thought he had over them.

"Isn't that amazing," she spit contemptuously. "You sit down to play cards and next thing you know, you've inherited someone's family."

He said nothing, just looked at her with his hazel eyes, so focused, so alert, so watchful.

"It doesn't make sense. None of this makes sense!" Sam crossed her arms over her chest, knuckles pressed to her ribs. "What do you want with us?"

"Maybe I'm a generous man with a sympathetic heart."

"Heart?" Sam heard the word burst from her lips, cold, icy. "No, I don't think that's it at all. There's something else happening here, something far more—" She broke off, bit back the word that crowded her mind. She couldn't say sinister in front of Gabby, couldn't alarm Gabby. Instead she shook her head, swallowed her fury and fear and reaching out, placed her hand protectively on the top of Gabby's head.

"I'm going to go upstairs," she said more calmly. "Check and see if Johann left me a note. I'm sure he did. I'm sure he'll have us join him as soon as he reaches wherever he's gone."

Cristiano's eyebrows lifted. "If you think so."

"I think so," she snapped, but of course she didn't think anything of the sort. She wouldn't be surprised if Johann had just fled. It was in his nature to run from problems.

Cristiano pursed his lips but held his tongue. He didn't think Johann was coming back. Not now. Not ever.

Sam hurried up the stairs with Gabby scampering at her side. Johann's room was dark and empty. Sam opened the closet, the four wide bureau drawers, and finally the small drawer in the night table but everything was empty save for a drawing Gabby had made him lying in the middle dresser drawer.

Sam took the crayon drawing out, looked at the picture which was one of the childish drawings where everyone is a stick figure either wearing a triangle dress or rectangle pants. The picture was meant to be Johann, Sam and Gabby all down at the beach, as if that was the way they were. A family.

They were no family. They'd never been a family, despite Sam's best efforts.

Sam didn't hear Cristiano come up behind her and when he spoke she jumped. "That's a lovely picture of the van Bergens on holiday," he said.

Eyes burning, face flushed, Sam quickly folded the picture and put it in the pocket of her lavender cardigan. It was that or cry, and she wouldn't cry, hated crying, having spent far too many years as a little girl in tears. If she'd learned anything, it was to present a confident face to the world. No one needed to know what she was thinking, or feeling. No one needed to know the truth. "Gabby's a very talented artist."

"And optimistic," he added mockingly.

She was just turning to walk out when she spotted an envelope on the bed, propped against Johann's pillow. Her name was written on the envelope.

Her hand shook ever so slightly as she ripped the envelope open and shook the papers out. Birth certificate, and a paper-clipped set of legal documents slid out. The birth certificate and papers were Gabriela's.

He was leaving her, Sam thought, suppressing horror even as it mixed with hope.

She unfolded the note, read Johann's wildly slanted scrawl.

Sam, I'm finished, gone, going home to Vienna. I thought together we had a good chance to beat Bartolo, but the game's up. Bartolo plays to win, and he's won. If it's any consolation, Gabby's yours. You know better what to do with her than me. I've lost it all now. Best of luck. You'll need it.
Johann van Bergen.

"What is that?" Cristiano asked.

A miracle, Sam thought, heart racing, eyes stinging. She blinked, turned the note around, held it up for him to see. "Read it."

He did, then silently handed it back.

"She's mine." Sam said quietly, fierccly, heart so full of emotion she wasn't even thinking. Just feeling. Gabby, gorgeous little Gabby was finally safe, finally hers, finally out of harm's way.

All these years…

All the worrying, the struggling, the praying. She'd prayed for a miracle and she'd finally got one.

Gabby was hers. Johann had left and left Gabriela Grace to Sam.

"So what happens now, Mr. Bartolo?" she asked, knowing this had to change things, knowing he couldn't possibly take both of them. It made no sense. He wouldn't want them both. Obviously other plans had to be made.

He shrugged. "We have tea."

"Now?"

"Then we'll get you settled at the Hotel de Paris until we make more permanent arrangements."

"So Gabby goes with me?"

His eyes narrowed fractionally. "For now."

Sam shot Gabby a protective glance but the little girl had left the room, wandering down to her own bedroom. "She's mine."

Sam's voice dropped, her inflection hard, flinty. "We stay together. Like it or not."

They had tea at the Hotel de Paris restaurant, Cote Jardin, a virtual indoor garden and terrace with a spectacular view of the harbor.

The service wasn't slow, but for Sam every moment felt endless. It didn't help, either, that their meal was interrupted repeatedly by strangers who stopped at their table to wish Cristiano well.

Although polite, Cristiano didn't encourage conversation and when the strangers moved on, didn't explain what he'd done to earn such enthusiastic well wishes. But after the last couple moved on, Sam wanted to know more.

"So you live here in Monaco?" she asked, stirring milk into her tea.

"I have a penthouse here, yes."

"But this isn't your primary home?"

The corner of his mouth curled. "I split my time evenly among my different residences."

She glanced at Gabby who was glued to the window watching the boats enter and leave the harbor. "How many residences?"

His smile deepened. "Enough that I never get bored."

Sam set her spoon in the saucer with an irritated clink. "Do you enjoy being enigmatic?"

"Not at all. I don't know what you want to know."

"I want to know everything."

"Everything?"

He was smiling again and she didn't understand it. Everything she said seemed to make him smile. How could she possibly be so amusing? "Yes, everything. I want to know where you live. I want to know what you do. I want to know who you are, how you spend your free time, the kind of friends you have."

"A character assessment."

"Yes."

He shrugged, leaned back in his chair, the sunlight playing

across his features, intensifying the green in his hazel eyes. "I can't do that for you. You'll have to use your own judgment regarding my character, but I can tell you basic things. I live here and on the Côte d'Azur. I have a home in Brazil on the coast but I don't go there often anymore. I have my own company. I'm successful and financially solvent. Is that what you want to know?"

No. That wasn't what she wanted to know. She didn't care about his things, she wasn't the least bit materialistic, and it annoyed her how easily people were impressed by money.

Money was useful, bought things, made certain decisions easier—even more convenient—but money as an end to a means? No. Never. Money ruined people. Changed everything. Sam didn't know if it was greed or a weakness in human nature, but too many people respected—admired—the wealthy simply because they were wealthy and had fatter bank accounts. But fat bank accounts don't make a person interesting and fat bank accounts don't make a person kind, considerate—valuable.

Sam glanced at Gabriela who was now talking to the waitress and pointing out something she'd seen in the harbor. "It's not your bank account that interests me, Mr. Bartolo, it's your heart. And that's what worries me. I don't know if you have one."

"I don't know, either," he agreed mockingly. "But hearts are overrated. Far better to be coldly pragmatic, to do what needs to be done, rather than what one feels like doing."

Sam's head shot up. "And what does that mean?"

"You feel attached to Gabby, so you've laid claim to her, but think about it: you've no legal claim to her, no biological tie—"

"Johann wants me to raise her."

"Does that make it right?"

"Yes."

"What about her mother's family? Wouldn't a blood relative be better than a stepmother?"

"Love isn't about biological ties."

"No?"

"No." Sam stared at him, hating him. He had a beautiful face, a face of a fallen angel, and yet his heart was so black and self-ish. "I love Gabriela and she loves me. Love is a gift. You can't buy it, win it, or barter it. I wouldn't trade her love for anything in the world."

"Not even three million pounds?"

"Are you trying to be funny? Because I find that rather insensitive considering our situation."

Cristiano's hazel eyes narrowed, lashes dropping, concealing his expression but from the tilt of his lips she could see he was amused. "You know, Baroness, there are many funny people in England. The greatest comics are all British and I've watched every Monty Python movie that exists. But you, sadly, lack a sense of humor."

"What about our situation do you find amusing?" She demanded tersely, refusing to acknowledge that he'd hit a sore spot. She'd never been able to laugh at herself. There hadn't been a lot of fun in her life growing up, or many occasions to tease and play. Life for an orphan was serious. "Our lives are changed forever and you're making jokes!"

"Not all change is bad, Baroness."

"In this case it is." Sam clasped her hands together in an effort to stay calm. "Please don't move us from the villa. Please don't take Gabby from the only home she knows."

"It's not much of a home."

Sam's cheeks burned, her temper spiking. "That's *not* the point."

Cristiano looked at her, long and level. "Then perhaps it should be." Abruptly he signaled to the passing maître d'hôtel that he wanted the bill. "Let me see you to my suite and then I'll work on locating Johann."

Still feeling feverish, her gaze met his. "And just what do you intend to do with a woman and her little girl? Use us as a tax write-up? Fight some archaic inheritance law?"

"I think you're actually trying to be funny." He dropped cash on the table and stood. "Shall we go?"

"You didn't answer my question."

"I don't think I have to."

She wasn't going to budge, wouldn't leave until he gave her a straight answer. She was sick of being pushed and pulled and jerked around. "What are you going to do with us?" she repeated in a low, unrelenting voice.

He stood over her, gazed down at her. "I'm going to find Johann—"

"Why?"

"I want to make sure everything's legitimate."

"He gave me her papers, wrote a note—"

"And I can't help wondering if it's all legal? Can one just really give away a child like that?" Cristiano's brow creased, his eyes narrowed. "First he tries to gamble Gabby, and then he abandons her. Seems highly suspect if you ask me."

His answer stayed with Sam, haunted Sam as he led them to the elevator that whisked them to his hotel suite.

It didn't matter what Cristiano found out. She wouldn't give Gabby back to Johann. She wouldn't give Gabby to anyone. Gabby was hers. She needed someone who loved her. Period.

Cristiano gave them a brief tour of the suite, pointing out the two bedrooms with ensuite baths, the sitting room connecting the two bedrooms, the small bar and refrigerator in the sitting room where they'd find cold drinks and other refreshments. "You'll be comfortable here," he said, with a glance at his watch. "Watch movies, television, whatever you like while I return a few phone calls. Once I'm off the phone we'll proceed from there."

Sam watched as he shut his bedroom door and then without even hesitating, she went to the second bedroom where their suitcases had been delivered and then with suitcases in hand, hustled Gabby to the elevator.

Taxis were already lined up in front of the hotel and it took just minutes to be seated and off. And yet despite their quick departure, Sam still held her breath much of the trip to the Nice airport. It was essential they catch the next British Airways flight to London-Heathrow, and from there they'd connect to Manchester.

In the back of the taxi, Sam wrapped her arm more snugly around Gabby.

Hard to believe they were running away like this.

Even harder to believe she was really going back.

It had been eight years since she'd left Cheshire, eight years since she'd fled the Rookery determined to never return.

But what was the old expression? Desperate times called for desperate measures? Well, Sam was nothing if not desperate now.

They didn't reach Chester until very late that night. The taxi driver had tried to discourage them from traveling so late from Manchester to Chester, but Sam insisted. She didn't have enough money for a taxi ride and hotel. They had to go to Chester. They had nowhere to sleep.

"Your address," the taxi driver said as they approached Chester's city limits. "It's not in town, is it?"

"No. It's actually closer to the village of Upton. It's called the Rookery."

Sam saw the driver look into the rearview mirror, his eyes briefly meeting hers. "Isn't that the orphanage?"

"Yes."

"Right," the driver said more kindly. "I know the place."

Fifteen minutes later, the driver took a left at a lane cut between two dark overgrown hedges. It was a long private driveway and everything gave an impression of neglect with tall, dead straggly weeds lining the dirt road while the road itself was muddy and full of potholes.

The whole area looked terribly forlorn and unkempt, but as the car headlights shone on the Rookery at the end of the driveway, the neglect was even more apparent.

The Rookery's main hall dated back to the late seventeenth century, but through time and need, rooms and wings had been added to the original stone keep. Tonight the Rookery was dark, and the bright car beams bounced off the leaded windows on the second and third floors, while the first floor windows were all boarded over.

The taxi driver parked, but left the engine running. "It's vacant," he said.

Indeed, it was. No cars, no lights, no people, no sign of life anywhere.

"Were you expected?" he persisted.

Sam slowly shook her head, unable to find her voice. She'd counted on the Rookery, counted on Mrs. Bishop, the head housekeeper, and Mr. Carlton, the groundskeeper. She was certain they'd still be here. They'd been here forever. The Rookery was their home.

"Did you use to live here?" the driver asked, squinting up through his windshield to get a look at the rampart high above. It was the only feature of the old keep that remained. The rest had been softened and changed in renovations.

"Yes."

It was all Sam could say. It was impossible to say more. If Charles had lived, things would have been different, of course, but Charles hadn't lived and now the Rookery was closed, and she and Gabby had no money and nowhere to go.

Which meant they'd stay here. She'd find a way in, or better yet, try to break into the gamekeeper's cottage to the far left of the old hall.

"So where can I take you?" The driver asked. "Into Chester? There's some decent hotels and inns in town."

Sam shook her head, opened the car door. "No, thank you. We'll be staying here."

The driver shook his head, obviously not pleased with her decision, but unwilling to intervene. He accepted his payment and drove away and as the taxi disappeared down the driveway, and Gabby shivered next to her, Sam realized just how late, and cold, and dark it was.

She'd made a mistake coming here. She should have gone with the taxi while they could.

But it was too late for regrets or remorse. They needed to get inside the gamekeeper's cottage and once inside, Sam would build a fire and they'd be warm.

The old stone cottage was tucked to the left of the Rookery, and although small, contained two bedrooms, a simple kitchen and a great room with a large stone hearth. Sam knew it would be chilly inside the cottage—dark, too, because obviously there wasn't even electricity anymore—but surely there'd be candles or lanterns, something to provide light.

Standing on tiptoe, Sam reached above the door, felt for a key not expecting to find one, and yet to her surprise, her fingers brushed cold metal. Thank God. The cottage key's hiding place had at least remained the same. Sliding the key off the door frame, Sam tried the dead bolt and it turned.

"We're in," Sam said, forcing cheer into her voice. "Let's see if I can't make us a proper fire now."

Nearly two hours later Sam was still trying to make a fire—she couldn't find matches in the dark, couldn't find anything to give her light—but thankfully Gabriela had fallen asleep on the old feather-stuffed couch, wrapped in thick blankets. At least Gabby was warm, Sam thought with a sigh as she sat back on her heels.

She was still contemplating the cold black hearth when she heard the purr of a motor outside, and then saw the wide arc of headlights flash through the dark cottage's unshuttered windows.

Someone was here.

But Sam felt anything other than relief as she heard the car come to a stop, the headlights shining directly on the small neglected cottage. This wasn't the taxi driver returning to check on them. And no one knew they were coming here.

Nervous, Sam went to the window overlooking the driveway. The car out front was a large sedan, a dark colored Mercedes. None of the locals who'd worked at the orphanage would drive a Mercedes, and to reach the Rookery, one had to drive a good quarter of a mile off the main road. Besides, it was late now, close to midnight.

Sam's fingers curled into her palms. This was no accidental call. Heart in her mouth she watched the door on the driver's side swing open. Cristiano Bartolo stepped out.

Sam stared at his tall shadowy figure in disbelief. It wasn't possible. It couldn't be possible. Despite the distance, the flights, the taxis and the borders, he'd found them already. It'd taken him just hours.

CHAPTER FOUR

LOCKED inside the cottage, Sam listened as he knocked once on the cottage door, then twice.

Three times.

And each time he knocked, it was harder, louder.

She glanced back to the living room where Gabriela still slept, but if Cristiano continued pounding on the door, he'd wake her soon.

"Open the door, Baroness." Cristiano's deep voice, although muffled by the dense wood door, still reached her.

He sounded angry. Angrier than she'd ever heard him. In Monte Carlo he'd been cynical, mocking, terse—but never angry.

He must have leaned closer to the door because when he spoke next, his voice was perfectly clear. "I'll give you to the count of three before I break the door down."

She said nothing. He had to be bluffing. The door was thick, old, it would be impossible to break down.

"Baroness, I don't make promises I don't keep. Keep that in mind as I start counting."

A shiver raced down her spine as she stood in the dark icy cottage. She craved light, and heat, craved safety but there was no safety for them now, not with Cristiano Bartolo on the other side of the door.

"*One.*"

Sam held her breath, nerves stretched to a breaking point.

"*Two.*"

"Wait!" Sam pressed her face to the door. "You can't break the door. It's hundreds of years old. It's been here longer than any of us has been alive—"

"Then open it now, before I say three."

Hell. Sam's hands trembled as she struggled to unbolt the lock, but it wasn't just her hands that shook as she swung the door open. The cold air rushed at her, surprised her. She hadn't realized the temperature had dropped so low.

"What are you doing here?" Sam faced Cristiano on the step outside. Moonlight outlined his profile, lit his dark hair, and yet it was his features that captured her attention. His jaw jutted, his full mouth pressed thin, and his dark eyes blazed. He was very unhappy with her at the moment.

Cristiano gave her a long hard look. "That's a silly question."

"You better go before I call the police."

"You don't have a phone, Baroness. And apparently, you haven't any gas or electricity."

He'd already figured that out, had he?

Sam shivered, hugged her arms closer to her chest. "You have a phone, and I'll call the police."

"Good. And then we can have a nice little chat with your Cheshire police about child smuggling."

"Child smuggling! I have her passport, her birth certificate—"

"That doesn't give you permission to take her out of the country. You're not her legal guardian yet. You haven't gone through the proper channels at all. The fact is, you broke so many international laws, Baroness, you'll be spending years behind bars. Now, move."

He was tall, so tall, that she had to tip her head back to see his face. "No."

He didn't even hesitate. "Then I'll let myself in."

Cristiano stretched an arm over her head, pushed the door open and lifting her in one arm, carried her into the cottage where he kicked the door shut and dropped her none too gently onto her feet. "Where is she?"

"Who?"

In the dim light she could see his expression and it wasn't pleasant. "For an intelligent woman, you're shockingly naïve."

He gave her yet another shadowy, contemptuous look. "I'm here, Baroness, in your Cheshire cottage. I've traveled the same route you did, having spoken with numerous people at airport ticket counters. So where is she?"

Sam swallowed, nodded with her head. "On the couch in there. She fell asleep while I tried to get the fire going."

"Which you couldn't do."

"I couldn't find matches in the dark."

"So what was your plan? To stay out here and freeze?"

Sam looked away, rightly chastened. It had been foolish coming here. Foolish and dangerous. "I'd hoped in the morning to find the matches."

"And what were you going to eat? I'm certain you haven't gone to a store for groceries."

"No."

He shook his head, looked as if he'd say more but changed topics. "Have you a fire laid then?" he asked, peeling off his coat.

"Yes. Logs and kindling."

Aided by moonlight, he walked into the main room with its great stone hearth. The cottage was several hundred years old, with a low, beamed ceiling that once warm, kept it snug. Crouching next to the hearth, he shifted some of the split logs around, piled the dry kindling higher at the base of the logs then used a lighter from his pocket to spark the kindling.

It took a few minutes before the kindling really caught, but soon the fire was blazing. Sam gratefully held her hands to the fire's heat. "It was cold," she confessed. "And I was worried. Thank you."

"You can ask for help," he said.

Her head lifted and she shot him a dubious look. "From you?" She rubbed her hands together before extending them again over the flickering gold flames. "The one that intended to return Gabby to Johann?"

"I didn't say I'd return her. I said I'd do what's right."

"You must see that having Johann look after Gabby isn't right. You must see that for yourself, you must see what he is—"

"I do."

Her gut burned. "Then spare her heartbreak. You don't have to care about me, or my feelings, but care about Gabriela's feelings. Please don't hurt her."

"I won't."

"You don't think taking a child from her home isn't traumatic?"

"But haven't you just done the same? Haven't you taken her from Monaco, the only home she's ever known, dragged her across the English Channel, plopped her in a car, driven her for miles to where? Chester? Upton? Wherever we are?" He shook his head, expression grim. "From her perspective, this frozen gray place must seem like Timbuktu."

"It's England, not Timbuktu."

"For an Italian child it's the same thing."

Sam stood, straightened. "Her mother was Spanish, not Italian."

"Catalonian, actually." Cristiano's lashes dropped, concealing his dark eyes. "And I knew her mother quite well, so let's avoid a who-knows-more competition."

They were both sitting close to the fire, speaking in hushed voice but this last pulled Sam up short, and she stared at Cristiano, mouth open. "You knew her mother?"

"Yes."

Sam sucked in air, a great gulp but it didn't fill her lungs, didn't help, did nothing to dull the throbbing in the back of her head. "Before Johann?"

"Yes."

Sam couldn't look away from Cristiano's taut features. "What happened?"

"Life happened." His expression was utterly blank, no emotion in his face or tone. "Gabriela's mother moved on. But that's not the issue now. The issue is you, running away with Gabriela—"

"I took her on a trip. I can do that. I'm her stepmother."

"That's right. Baroness van Bergen." And he smiled, his teeth flashing white, but it was such a hard, unforgiving smile that Sam shivered inwardly.

Cold or fear, she wondered? Or maybe it was more dread, because that's what filled her stomach in hard heavy bricks. "I wish you wouldn't call me Baroness anymore."

"What then?"

"Samantha will do."

Cristiano's head tipped and in the yellow-gold light of the fire he studied her through narrowed eyes. "You're such a contradiction, Samantha. On one hand, you're so very prim and proper, and then on the other you've this fierce spirit—"

"Can you tell me more about Gabriela's mother? Gabby used to ask about her. I never knew what to tell her."

"She was a film actress."

"Not that. More like, her personality. What was she like?"

"Mercedes?" He paused, reflected. "Beautiful. Lively. She was a great deal of fun."

"Is Gabby very like her?"

"I think Gabby's a mix of her mother and father."

Sam turned, looked at Gabby where she slept on the couch cocooned in blankets. "I've wished for years that Gabriela had a different life. I've wished it were more stable, more predictable. I tried to give her everything. It's one thing for an adult to struggle, but it's another for a child."

"Has Gabriela suffered?"

"I'm sure she has. We both have to a greater or lesser extent. There's never enough money. Johann's rarely home. He may be Gabby's father, but he's shown her little love and even less attention."

"Was he so different before you married him?"

"No."

Cristiano watched her. "But you thought you'd marry him anyway, marry into a life of privilege?"

"It's never been a very privileged life. I worked hard."

"And I bet you just hated being a baroness."

"Yes, I did. It was false."

"False?"

"Johann didn't love me and I didn't love him. It was a marriage of convenience, that and nothing more."

"Nothing more?"

Her own lips curved, in an equally hard cynical smile. She'd changed so much since Charles died, he wouldn't even recognize her if he was alive now. "Nothing more." Shivering, she held her hands up to the flames to try to warm herself. "I was convenient to marry."

She leaned closer, stared into the flickering fire with its red and gold flames feeling the weight of years of secrets and silence on her. "You see, Mr. Bartolo, before I was the baroness, I was the van Bergens' nanny."

"The nanny?" He sounded shocked.

Sam looked at him, lips twisting wryly. "I've never told anyone before. Johann forbid me from telling people. He didn't want anyone to know I'd been the hired help, but in private he never let me forget. It was one of the ways he ridiculed me—I was just a working girl, not an aristocrat like him."

"You should have left him," Cristiano said flatly.

"And what? Leave Gabby?" Sam drew a breath, her chest tender and glanced down at her hands bare of any rings. Johann had bought her a ring but he'd asked for it back when money got tight. "I couldn't do that. Not then, not now, not ever."

"Why are you so devoted?"

"I don't know. I suppose Gabby needed someone to love her, and I—" She broke off, aware of how close she came to saying the words, and *I needed someone to love*. She finished the thought differently. "I like to be useful."

"Johann found you useful?"

"I did what he needed me to do."

"Including keeping Mercedes's family away."

Sam winced. "A mistake. I thought I was keeping a family together. I thought I'd be a good wife." *A good mother.*

His eyes, dark in the firelight, met hers and for a long unblinking moment he just looked at her, as if he could see into her. "We all make mistakes," he said at last.

Something in his voice nearly moved her to tears. He sounded almost sympathetic and that was unbearable. She bunched her hands in her lap, fighting emotions she didn't know how to manage. Her life, like Gabby's, hadn't been easy, and in her life there had been few people looking out for her. Just Charles, and then Charles was gone as suddenly as he'd come into her life.

"Whatever happens," she said hoarsely, thinking she shouldn't have come back to the Rookery, shouldn't have returned here at all. "Do not pity us. We don't need your pity."

"I don't think I mentioned pity."

Her teeth scraped together. She dropped her voice lower. "Maybe not. But I can see what you're thinking."

He dropped his voice even lower and leaning forward, he caught her chin in his hand, tilting her face up to his. "Then I need to buy you some glasses, Samantha, because apparently you can't see a damn thing. You can't see what's in front of you— good or bad—and that's a problem. Not just for you, but Gabriela."

His hand burned where it touched her chin, her skin flaming hot, hotter. His touch was firm, sure, a finger at her chin, his thumb beneath, close to her throat. She shuddered a little. Everything was wrong. Nothing was right anymore. Her entire world had upended and she felt as if she were standing on top of her head. "I didn't think you cared about Gabriela."

Abruptly he released her, sat back. "It's late," he said shortly, "nearly two in the morning. We'll talk more in the morning."

She nodded, confused by his rapid mood change but too worried about antagonizing him to ask for an explanation. "There are two bedrooms, but they'll both be cold."

"Are the beds made up?" he asked, standing.

"Yes. There are extra quilts in chests at the foot of each bed."

"Which room is yours?"

"It doesn't matter. I'm just going to sleep in here near Gabby."

He started to leave and then stopped in the shadowed hall. "Maybe you weren't the wife you hoped you'd be, but surely Johann wasn't the husband you'd hoped for, either."

Sam's eyes burned. She'd never admit it to Cristiano, but she hadn't really expected much from Johann. She'd worked for him before they'd married. She knew who he was, and what he was, and maybe that's why she accepted his proposal. It was a paper marriage, was meant to be a loveless marriage. She knew she'd never love anyone the way she'd love Charles…and quite frankly, didn't think she deserved love after losing Charles.

"Isn't there a saying," she said softly as the fire fizzed and popped, "be careful what you wish for?" Sam looked up, met Cristiano's hooded gaze. "It's true. I learned that one the hard way, too." She grimaced, wrapped her arms tighter around her knees. "Anyway, it is late. Good night. Sleep well."

Cristiano was right, morning did come early, but the fire never died out and Sam found out later, when she woke, it was because Cristiano had gotten up repeatedly during the night to add more logs to keep the cottage warm.

Gabby, for her part, was delighted to discover they had company. "You!" she said, bounding out of her bed on the couch as she spotted Cristiano entering the house, carrying a stack of firewood. "You came to see us in England!"

"I did."

Gabby grabbed one of the blankets and wrapped it around her shoulder as he stacked the split logs next to the hearth. "You played cards with Papa."

Sam turned sharply towards Gabby. "How do you know that?"

"He did, didn't he?" she asked innocently. "And he took Papa's money, too."

"Gabriela!"

The girl looked from one to the other. "Didn't he?"

Cristiano tossed a log onto the fire. "Yes," he said bluntly as sparks hissed and shot from the fire. "He wasn't a very good cardplayer."

Gabby nodded thoughtfully and she chewed her lip. "That's what Sam says, too." And then her expression cleared. "Maybe you can play some cards with me."

Sam nearly choked on her tongue. "I don't think he plays the kind of games we play, Gabriela."

"I can teach him," Gabby answered. "Go Fish and War is easy."

"I think I remember how to play." Cristiano smiled faintly as he brushed his hands off. "In fact, I used to be very good at War."

"Really?" Gabby's tongue poked out, touched the corner of her mouth giving her a slightly naughty look. "I bet I'm better than you." She leaned forward, said in a stage whisper. "I beat Sam. I beat everyone."

Sam blushed with embarrassment but Cristiano laughed, a deep masculine sound that rumbled from his chest.

"You are your father's child, aren't you?" he said, but he wasn't looking at Gabby as he spoke. He was looking right at Sam.

And suddenly Sam understood even though she didn't want to. Last night she'd ignored the facts, but this morning she couldn't play ostrich. It was all beginning to make sense. The card games, the high stakes, the ruthless moves, the seizing of family and assets…

She was forced to ask questions now, forced to piece it together bit by bit.

Perhaps this wasn't just a gambler's impulse move…

Perhaps all along Cristiano had ulterior motives…

Perhaps Cristiano, not Johann, was Gabriela's father…

But those fragmented thoughts were forgotten as Gabby scrambled to the window and announced, "Someone's coming! It's a lady and she looks mad."

Sam tucked a blond curl behind her ear and exchanging swift glances with Cristiano, headed for the door. But on opening the door, Sam froze as she caught sight of the white-haired woman bundled in a thick gray wool. "Mrs. Bishop," she whispered, rooted to the spot.

The elderly woman looked equally stunned, her annoyance giving way to shock. "Samantha?"

Sam closed the distance and gave the older woman a swift hug. "What are you doing here?"

Mrs. Bishop clasped her hands on Sam's shoulders. "I should ask you the same! You gave us all quite a scare. I'd heard there were lights here last night, and I insisted Gilbert, my son-in-law, drive me over." She paused, tilted her head back, searched Sam's face. "It's been so long, my girl. Where have you been?"

"Away." Sam tried to smile but couldn't. Suddenly the past was rushing back, painful memories she didn't want, couldn't bear. Charles had died eight years ago and yet suddenly it seemed as if it were just yesterday. "How is everyone? And where is everyone? When did the Rookery close?"

"Not long after you left."

"I see." Sam bit her lip, and she did see, she knew exactly what had happened. Without Charles to run things there probably wasn't funding, or the management, to keep the orphanage open. "Would you come in?"

Mrs. Bishop nodded, and followed Sam back into the cottage but her expression fell as she took in the cottage's deplorable conditions. "You can't possibly mean to stay here. The cottage is a wreck. There's no water, heat, plumbing. What are you thinking?"

Sam smiled, but tears filled her eyes. "I don't know."

Mrs. Bishop saw the tears and shaking her head, clucked, "It's not been easy, has it, my girl?"

Mrs. Bishop's kindness would be Sam's undoing and yet Sam knew she couldn't break down here, not in front of Gabby, not with Cristiano standing just a stone's throw away, listening to everything being said. Which reminded her, she ought to make introductions. She couldn't very well pretend Gabby and Cristiano weren't here.

But Mrs. Bishop had spotted Gabby already. She clapped her hands, bent low. "And is that your little girl?"

Gabby scampered to Sam's side. "Um, yes." Sam put an arm around Gabby's shoulders. "I'm her...her...nanny."

"And my mum. My stepmum," the little girl corrected. "You

see, she married my dad. Johann van Bergen. But he left us. There were problems with money."

Mrs. Bishop's head shot up and she stared aghast at Sam. "Is this true?"

Sam flushed. "More or less."

"And is that why you're here?" Mrs. Bishop continued worriedly. "You've nowhere else to go?"

Put like that it sounded absolutely appalling. A desperate Sam dragging a little girl across the continent to a derelict orphanage in Cheshire.

Her mouth opened, her throat worked, but there was no ready answer. Just the sting of tears she wouldn't cry, and the bite of memory, the ache of heartbreak.

She'd grown up here, gone to school here, and would have lived here as Charles's wife if he hadn't died. No wonder she'd run here when she didn't know where to go. Until she was eighteen, the Rookery was her entire world.

"We're in transition," she said, finally finding her voice. "But I thought until we were more settled, it'd be nice to visit."

Mrs. Bishop's light blue gaze, though watery, missed little. "Are you in trouble, my girl?"

Sam's cheeks burned and she shook her head swiftly and before she could stumble her way through another feeble protest, Cristiano moved forward.

"Samantha wanted us to see her home," he said, sliding an arm around Sam, his hand resting lightly, and yet provocatively, on her hip. "She thought it was important we knew where she came from."

"Yes, of course." Mrs. Bishop was nodding and clucking again. "You've heard then all about her life. So much tragedy for one so young." She regarded Sam with a look of tenderness. "I was the head housekeeper when she came to stay with us at the Rookery. It was a very difficult time but we loved her and she adjusted, although there were many nights we heard her crying."

"*Mrs. Bishop,*" Sam remonstrated, going hot and cold. Mrs.

Bishop's shared memories were nearly as painful as Cristiano's arm against her lower back, his hand warm on her hip, her body exquisitely sensitive.

"I know it's hard, Samantha," Mrs. Bishop said, reaching out to touch Sam's cheek. "But if he loves you half as much as we do, he'll want to know everything."

Sam shuddered. "He knows enough."

"So you've told him all about Charles, then?" Mrs. Bishop's expression gentled even more. "Ah, that was a tragedy no one's forgotten—"

"Mrs. Bishop." Sam's voice came out strangled.

But Mrs. Bishop so engrossed in her memories and stories seemed oblivious to Sam's agony. "It was horrific. No one could believe it, no one knew what to do. Our beautiful Sam, a bride and a widow all in the same night."

CHAPTER FIVE

THE silence that followed didn't last long, no more than any other silence following a difficult remark, but for Sam, it felt endless.

She'd never told anyone about Charles, had never spoken about her brief marriage that ended less than eight hours after the ceremony.

Sam stepped away from Cristiano. "With the Rookery closed, where do you live now, Mrs. Bishop?" Her voice was crisp, and she did her best to look firmly in control. Best thing to do now was quickly move forward. Act as if nothing had been said. "I know you had family in the area."

Sam succeeded in distracting the elderly woman and Mrs. Bishop nodded. "That's right. I broke my hip a number of years ago and it's slowed me so I live with my daughter, and her family now." Mrs. Bishop glanced down at Gabriela. "In fact, I have several granddaughters very close to your age. They're twins."

Gabby beamed. "I'm almost five. I'll be five February 16th."

"Well today is Saturday, the perfect day for a tea party."

Sam smiled, smoothed Gabriela's dark hair back from her brow. "That sounds like fun. Maybe later Gabby can meet the girls."

"Why doesn't she come home with me now?" Mrs. Bishop said stoutly.

"We haven't even had breakfast." Sam felt the panic return,

the sensation like little needles in her stomach and brain. She couldn't be alone with Cristiano, couldn't be here with Cristiano, didn't want Gabby gone and Cristiano looking at her, talking to her, having anything to do with her.

Mrs. Bishop waved away the protest. "She can have breakfast with the girls, and we're just down the lane, not even a mile away. If she wants to come home, we'll call you and zip her right back."

"Can I go?" Gabby tugged on Sam's hand. "Can I? I bet they have dolls and lots of toys."

And gazing down into Gabriela's eager little face, Sam realized all over again how much Gabriela had been deprived of these past four and a half years. Not just toys and pretty dresses, but parties and playdates. Friends. Johann wouldn't let anyone ever come to the house, and overtures made by parents at Gabriela's school had been immediately rebuffed by Johann. "You're not afraid to go?" Sam asked softly.

"No! I'm not afraid of anything."

It was true. Just last summer Gabby had leaped off the high dive at a local swimming pool—a diving board so high that most nine- and ten-year-old girls avoided it—but Gabby had loved it. Gabby said when she grew up she wanted to be an astronaut, or a fireman, as long as she could go fast and jump out of tall buildings.

Sam had never understood where Gabby got her thrill-seeking personality from, but now it was beginning to make sense.

Sam looked at Cristiano, hesitated. "You don't mind if she goes, do you?"

"Not if you're comfortable," he answered evenly. "And I can give Mrs. Bishop my mobile number. That way she can call the moment Gabriela gets tired or the girls stop having fun."

Sam nodded gratefully. "Good idea. Then we can just run down and pick her up."

"Or I can bring her back."

While Mrs. Bishop and Cristiano exchanged phone numbers, Sam went to locate Gabby's coat, and then using her fingers, did her best to comb Gabby's hair smooth before pulling it into a long ponytail. "Be good," Sam whispered into the little girl's ear, walking her from the primitive bathroom back to the cottage door. "Don't cause any trouble."

Gabby flashed an impish smile. "I never do!"

And it crossed Sam's mind, as Mrs. Bishop trundled a beaming Gabriela toward the car, that nothing must dim Gabriela's quick smile and bright eyes. Gabriela mustn't ever grow up quickly. She should remain a child as long as she was a child. Sam was only six when her own parents died and life had never been the same. Everyone at the Rookery had tried to step in, patch things together, but mothers and fathers were never replaced. And Sam's parents, although working class, had been solid and loving. Dependable.

And that's what Sam tried to be for Gabby. Solid, loving. Dependable.

As Mrs. Bishop shut her own door, she rolled down the window and leaned out. "Sam I nearly forgot. I have the key to the Rookery. Why don't you stay there? It has a generator in back, and a proper kitchen with working appliances."

"Oh, I don't know," Sam said, glancing at the cottage behind her. It was small, and rustic, but it was also quaint and cozy in a way the old rambling Rookery would never be.

"Take the key anyway." Mrs. Bishop extended her hand, held a key ring out to her. "Just return it to me when you leave."

Sam was conscious of Cristiano standing behind her as she stood in the driveway watching Mrs. Bishop slowly make her way down the lane, her small blue car bouncing in the potholes just like the taxi did last night. The lane was a mess, the sides of the road a jungle of weeds and blackberry thorns, so different from how Sam remembered it as a child.

"You don't let her out of your sight very much, do you?" Cristiano said, his voice a deep rumble.

Sam shivered at the bite of cold air. It was chillier this morning than it had been last night when they arrived. "No." Reluctantly she turned to face him, her hands burrowing in her coat pockets, fingers stiff. "I worry about her when she's gone."

"Why?"

"Things have happened in the past," she said evasively, unwilling to go into detail about the kidnapping attempt several years ago that had put Sam in the hospital and given Gabby nightmares for months. It had been three years since the kidnapping attempt—someone had obviously thought Baron van Bergen had more money than he did—but the terror was still very real to Sam.

She still didn't know who had targeted Gabriela, and the Monaco police had never come to any conclusions. In the end they concluded it was a random attack. They'd told Johann how lucky it was that Sam was there, and that she fought as hard as she did to defend Gabriela, otherwise the perpetrator would have succeeded.

But Sam didn't feel lucky. The police's conclusions did little to comfort Sam, and until the case was solved, Sam believed that Gabby remained a target.

"What things?" Cristiano asked.

Sam shrugged uncomfortably. She didn't like talking about bad things, didn't want to dwell on that which was frightening or out of her control. Funny, she thought, how much she didn't let herself think about, or feel. "Something happened years ago that's made me extra protective toward Gabby. Nothing's happened since, but I still worry."

Cristiano's brow furrowed and he looked down the lane where the blue car had gone and then back to Sam. "But you trust Mrs. Bishop?"

"Oh, yes." Sam mustered a smile, knowing she was being silly and yet old habits were so hard to break. "Mrs. Bishop was like a surrogate mother to me when I lived here—she'd do anything for me, and I know she'll take good care of Gabby. She's a very kind woman."

"So why are you so uneasy?"

Because I'm stuck with you, that's why.

He made her uneasy. There was no other way to put it. And she didn't want him here in the small cottage. She didn't want to be alone with him. He was too big, too intense, too different.

Her eyes met his, and as if he could read her mind, his lips curved in a faint sardonic smile. Heat exploded in Sam's middle, her face flaming, her limbs going weak.

She didn't like him. Didn't want to like him. Didn't want him anywhere near her, but somehow she knew he wasn't going away, and he wasn't going to be leaving her—or Gabby—alone.

"It's hard being back here," she said, as much as she could, or would say. If there's anything she'd learned it was the value of silence, of avoiding conflict and controversy. As a child she'd waited years to be adopted, hoping against hope that she'd someday be placed with a real family, praying she'd eventually be wanted somewhere. It never happened. But the years of trying so hard to please, the years of waiting to be accepted, wanted, adopted, had left a lasting impression. Don't make waves. Avoid conflict. Try to keep peace. Make others happy.

No wonder she became a professional nanny. The only thing she was good at was making others happy.

Sam squeezed her hand inside her pocket, the Rookery's key ring now warm in her palm. Again she wondered why she thought this was the right place to go. Again she regretted her decision to return.

"I would have thought you'd be anxious to leave this morning," she added, aware of Cristiano's scrutiny, knowing he was watching her, measuring, evaluating.

"I am. But there are things we should discuss, things Gabriela shouldn't hear. Now would be a good time for us to talk."

Sam nodded, doing her best to ignore the sense of trepidation weighting her limbs. Immediately she flashed to Johann and Mercedes, or was it Cristiano and Mercedes? Is that what Cristiano wanted to tell her? That he and Mercedes had been lovers? And if Gabby was his child, then what would happen next?

What would happen to *her?* Why had he bought *her?*

Cristiano suggested they drive into Chester, have breakfast and buy some groceries in case they stayed one more night.

"If we're to stay another night, shouldn't we stay in a hotel here in town?" Sam asked as they settled into a booth at a Chester restaurant, the ceiling low in the historic half-timbered building, the interior dark, the booths hard and high, uncomfortably like church pews.

Cristiano barely glanced at the menu before setting it aside. "And give you another chance to run away? I don't think so."

"You couldn't have been comfortable last night."

"That's kind of you to worry about me," he drawled, leaning back in the booth. "But it's not necessary. I may look delicate, but I'm surprisingly tough. And no, it wasn't the best night's sleep, but at least I knew where you were."

Sam felt heat creep up her neck, into her cheeks. "What if I promised you I wouldn't go anywhere—"

"Wouldn't believe you." He smiled at her but the smile was hard, fixed. "I don't trust you."

Her hands twisted beneath the table. "Anything I've done—"

"Yes, I know, you've done for Gabriela. But I don't buy that, Samantha. This is about you. You don't want to lose Gabriela. You don't want to be without her."

"And why should I be? I've spent years with her, years loving her."

"But you're not her mother, or her father. You're not her family—"

"Neither are you!"

His dark gaze held hers in a long, timeless moment. "Are you sure?"

Sam's stomach churned. It had come to this. No more running away from the inevitable.

"She's a Bartolo," he said, slowly, deliberately. "I've been trying to get her back for years."

"But the gambling...Johann..."

"Why would I buy her? She's mine, belongs with me. I knew if I took you Gabby would follow. I could have only taken Gabby if I destroyed Johann first."

"I don't believe it."

"Come on, Sam. Don't play ostrich now."

She sat still, one hand kneading the other, seeing but not seeing, thinking but not thinking. If what he said was true…if Gabriela were indeed his child…Sam had no place in Gabriela's life anymore. It was Gabby he'd wanted all along, not her. Johann's letter giving Gabby to her meant nothing. It was just another sick joke on his part. One last stab at her.

She felt close to throwing up.

Sam pressed a hand to her middle. "You've had a DNA test?"

"Yes."

Her mouth was so dry it hurt to swallow. "And the evidence?"

"Conclusive."

Dazed, she shook her head, unable to think clearly. Her thoughts were too wild, her fear and confusion too great. "But then, why isn't she with you? Why didn't the court appoint you her legal guardian?"

"The courts eventually will, but I don't want to wait any longer. My patience had run out. I've missed out on the first four and a half years of Gabby's life as it is. I won't miss any more."

A new thought came to her, a new, more frightening thought. She sat taller, stomach in knots. It took all of her courage to get the question out. "Were you behind the kidnapping attempt three years ago?"

"No."

But he knew about the attempt, she thought, heart racing. He wasn't surprised by her question. He was familiar with the incident. "What do you know?"

"I know you were hurt."

Sam looked at him quickly, and then away. "It wasn't that bad."

"You were in the hospital for a week."

She smiled grimly, remembering how Johann proposed while she was still in the hospital. Johann had said he needed her, and Gabby needed her and that by marrying him, Sam would make him a better man.

It didn't work out that way, of course. After the wedding, and as soon as Sam had fully recovered from the beating, she assumed even more household responsibilities than before. She wasn't just the nanny now, but the cook, the housekeeper, the bookkeeper, the gardener, the seamstress, the laundress because, Johann, citing financial difficulties, had let all hired help go.

"How did you find out?" she asked, knowing that even though the workload was exhausting, by that point she was so attached to Gabby that she couldn't imagine leaving.

"I've been keeping my eye on van Bergen."

She felt a shiver of apprehension. "You've been spying on us?"

Again he fell silent, and his silence was somehow more effective than other peoples' words. His silence conveyed tremendous strength and power, as well as calm. The word, unflappable, crossed her mind.

She looked at him where he sat across from her in the oak booth, his long legs out and braced before him, his hands resting lightly just below his hipbones. Something in his stillness, something in his pose—his hands resting just so—reminded her of a gunslinger from one of the old cowboy movies she used to watch with her father late at night when there was nothing else on the telly.

"I'd prefer to call it investigating," he said, speaking slowly, carefully. "I was intent on gathering facts. Evidence. Making sure Gabriela was safe until I could get her in my care."

"So you've tried going to court?"

"We've been in court for years—but it takes so long. I expect a legal decree soon—"

She felt dangerously close to hysteria. "So why the poker games?"

"Revenge." Cristiano's upper lip curled. "I wanted to make him suffer. He made me suffer. It seemed only fair."

"Suffering is never fair."

"You're such a good girl, Samantha."

She wouldn't be baited, not this time. "So I wasn't important. You never wanted me—"

"Not true." He cut her off. "I wanted you from the beginning. I gambled on the fact that once I had you, Gabriela would follow."

"That's illogical."

"Sam, you married Johann for Gabriela. If you came to me, you'd bring Gabriela. And I was right." He smiled at her but his smile was predatory. "You've protected her from the beginning. I don't hold that against you. In fact, I appreciate the fact that you love her for her—not for her bank account."

"She has a bank account?"

"A huge trust fund. She's a Bartolo."

"I don't know what that means."

Cristiano's lashes lowered and he studied her as though she were a curiosity, something he'd uncovered in a dusty secondhand shop. "It means she's rich. It means she will always wonder when she grows up if men love her for her, or if they love her money."

"That's horrible."

"That's reality."

She pursed her lips, trying to digest this and everything else she'd learned. "And that's what you want for her? Some harsh reality where her life is ruled by money, not love?"

"Sam, life is what it is. I'm not going to sugarcoat it for Gabriela, you, or anyone. But I've been observing Gabriela. She's a bright girl. She's confident and assertive. There's no reason she can't be rich, and be loved."

Somehow Sam felt the inequities very much. She—who'd tried so hard for so many years—had neither love nor money. "Do you have both? Are you rich?"

"Yes."

"Loved?"

He laughed, cool and mocking. "No. But that's my choice."

Sam had never met anyone like Cristiano Bartolo, didn't understand anyone like him, either. "Why wouldn't you want love?"

"Love's complicated. It involves layers of emotion including guilt and fear. I'm happier without it."

"Without love."

"As I said, I'm happy as I am."

She shook her head, perplexed. "So why do you want Gabby?"

He hesitated for the briefest second. "Because she's a Bartolo. She should be raised by a Bartolo."

He was making her sick. She couldn't stand his way of thinking. It was harsh, horrible, selfish. "This isn't why you take a child—"

"It is for me," he cut in sharply before lifting the menu. "Do you know what you're going to eat?"

Sam couldn't imagine eating a bite after that but when the waitress appeared at their table, she ordered toast and tea, thinking she had to put something in her stomach if she was going to survive the day.

They sat in virtual silence while they waited for their breakfast to arrive until Sam couldn't stand the miserable tension a moment longer. "So what are you going to do? How exactly does this work?"

"In the morning we'll fly back to Monte Carlo. On Monday Gabby will begin at her new school."

"A new school?"

"Yes."

Sam stared at him aghast. So upset she ignored the waitress when she brought Sam her pot of tea. "You're out of your mind." And he was. He had to be to think he could just rip Gabriela from everything she'd known and loved. "Maybe adults understand moves and shifts, maybe adults can be relocated overnight, but not children—"

"I'm not asking you, Samantha. I'm telling you this. The decision is made. It's no longer your concern."

She shuddered, knowing he was wrong, knowing Gabriela would always be her concern. She might not be her nanny anymore, might not even be her stepmother, but Gabby was part of her heart, her life. "What is the rush?"

"I've lost enough time trying to get her home. I refuse to lose anymore."

The hopelessness of the situation wrapped hard fingers

around Sam's throat. "And what about Gabby? What about all *she* loses?"

Cristiano's eyes narrowed. "She'll thank me one day."

"Maybe. And maybe not."

He shrugged. "I guess we'll find out."

Sam felt as if he were splitting her heart and head wide-open. How could he do this? How could he even talk this way? How was it possible to be so callous…much less about your own child? "Why can't you give her time," Sam pleaded. "At least let her finish the school year where she is. Don't change everything on her overnight. She's so young. She's been through so much. Give her time to understand what's happening…time to adjust."

He leaned back as their breakfast plates were carried to the table. "She'll have time," he said. "She'll have the next fifteen years to adjust."

She swayed on her seat. "What kind of man are you?"

His steady gaze held hers, and the way he studied her made her skin prickle, her body tingling with alarm. "The kind who gets what he wants."

"And what about what other people want?"

"Not my concern."

Sam's stomach rose, nearly upending. "God, that's cold."

"Yes, but damn practical."

Conversation finished, Cristiano concentrated on eating his bacon and egg breakfast while Sam tore apart her toast, heartsick.

Sitting there, Sam wished she could do something, wished she could intervene even as she'd foiled the kidnapping attempt three years ago by hurling herself at the kidnapper. She'd used her own body to shield Gabby, and it had worked. Sort of.

Sort of.

Sam's lower lip quivered and she bit into it ruthlessly. She wasn't going to let him see how much he upset her, wouldn't let him have the upper hand again.

She waited until he'd finished his meal and then gathered her coat and purse. "Can we go get Gabby now?"

"You haven't taken a bite of your toast."

"Not hungry," she answered, chilled on the inside. Three years ago she'd saved Gabby, three years ago she'd been brave, heroic. Why couldn't she find a way to save Gabby today?

It felt bitterly cold outside, the sky like an endless sheet of metal, and Sam shivered on the way to the shop where they bought milk, bread and groceries for dinner. It was a relief to reach the car, where Cristiano immediately turned on the heat. They didn't speak though, and as Cristiano drove, Sam stared intently out the window, trying not to obsess about Cristiano's plans for Gabriela, but it was impossible to think of anything else.

"I'll need your help," he said abruptly. "I brought the school admissions packet with me, and there's quite a long list of things she'll need. Proper uniform, wardrobe, essentials."

"Cristiano."

"I'd initially planned on leaving her in her current school," he continued as though she'd never spoken. "But I was naïve. I thought you could continue taking her to school in the morning, and then picking her up again after, but obviously that's not going to work, not if I can't trust you with her."

"You can."

"I can't, and I travel a great deal with my work. Which is why I've decided the best place for her is Ludwin's—"

"Ludwin's? That's a boarding school!"

"One of the best in Europe. The waiting list is long. I was lucky they accepted her."

Sam leaned forward to get a good look at his expression, thinking he was joking, thinking he had to be joking. "Gabby's not even five yet."

"She'll be five next month."

"Yes, and she thinks she's having a circus party and has been helping me plan it."

"I'll take her to the Monte Carlo's Royal Circus instead."

Sam's mouth opened, closed. She couldn't make a sound. How could he even consider sending her away? "Have you looked at her, Cristiano? She's a tiny thing still. Far too young for boarding school. She could be picked on by other children, tormented, and then all the rules, the infractions and punishments—"

"It'll toughen her up."

Tears burned the back of her eyes. "*No*. Toughening up isn't what you think it is. Toughening up is having your heart broken and your hopes shattered. Toughening up breaks a child down before it builds her up. Don't do it to her, Cristiano."

"I've been to boarding school. I survived."

"Yes, survived. But surviving isn't living. I know. My parents died when I was six. I grew up in a boarding school for orphans. That's what the Rookery is. A place where children live because they have nowhere else to go, but Gabby has somewhere to go. She has you, she has me—"

"You're not part of the equation anymore, Samantha." He shot her a hard look. "I don't trust you."

Cristiano felt a twinge of remorse as Sam blanched, her face paling, her eyes huge and dark with pain. He didn't enjoy hurting women and children. He was a competitor, a fighter, but not malicious, especially not toward those weaker.

He could see the effect his words were having on her. She was in torment, but it was the same torment he'd known these past four and a half years as he battled to get Gabriela back. At first he'd tried to go the legal route, do everything above-board, but Johann had blocked his every move, dragging the custody battle into an endless tangle of court appearances and appointments. He wanted to get his hands on Gabby's money.

"So why did you want me," she whispered, looking at him, her blue eyes bruised, her expression wounded. "Why take me from Johann?"

He hesitated for a split second, then realized at the very least, he owed her an honest answer. "There were three reasons. One, I knew wherever you went, Gabby would go. Two, you're the one that's kept me from Gabby—"

"Me?"

"If you hadn't married Johann, Gabby would have been mine years ago."

"I didn't know—"

"It doesn't matter." The years of waiting for Gabby, and the endless legal wrangling, had taken a toll on his patience. He was done with playing nice. Done with accommodating others at his—or Gabriela's—expense. "Fortunately I have her back now and I'll do what needs to be done."

"Do you love her?"

"She's my family. She's a Bartolo." He was determined to make Samantha understand she wasn't in charge of Gabriela's future any longer. She had to accept him as Gabby's guardian.

"You know her sizes," he continued calmly. "I'll give you the list Ludwin's sent me, all her requirements are there. I imagine she'll want something from home for comfort, too. A blanket or stuffed animal. If Gabby has one—"

"She has a doll she loves."

"Then send that with her."

"You'll crush her, Cristiano." Sam's voice broke, her words all but inaudible. "She's a little girl that's lost her mother, and the man she thinks is her father. How can boarding school with Spartan dormitories be the answer?"

"The school has an impressive reputation. They've assured me they'll do everything in their power to help her adjust."

"But they don't know Gabby, or care about her. But I do. And I know you must or you wouldn't have worked so hard to get her back." Tears shimmered in her eyes. "Hate Johann, hate me, hate our lives, the world we inhabit, the truth, the lies, but don't play God, and you can't say you aren't when you're already planning on sending her away."

"But what are my options? I can't leave her with you—not if I can't trust you."

"But you can. I'm telling you. I'm making a promise—"

"I can trust that?"

"Yes."

He was silent, then sighed. "I wish I could believe you, but I can't. I was lucky you came here, fortunate you brought her to Chester. I knew from the private investigator's report that you'd been raised in Cheshire. He said if you ever ran away, you'd probably return here, but in the future you won't come here. And then what? Where do I find Gabriela then?"

"I won't take her away from you. I promise."

He steeled himself against the anguish in her voice, refusing to let her needs usurp his own.

Sam still pleaded her case. "I'm an honest person, and fair, Cristiano. If I give you my word—" Her voice broke and she pressed her hands together against her chest, held them there as though her heart hurt. "I'm as straight as they come. If you take the time to get to know me, you'll see I'm trustworthy."

He couldn't look at her, couldn't let the agony in her voice touch him. She was emotional now, but later she'd see that he was right. Later, when she remarried and had a family of her own, she'd be grateful he'd taken Gabriela back. "Forgive me, but you know the expression, once bitten, twice shy."

She ducked her head but he saw the first tear fall. *"Please."*

Don't think about her, he told himself, don't look at her. This isn't about her. It's about family, his family, the family that didn't exist anymore. Gabby was all there was left. Gabby was the last Bartolo. He had to have her back. He needed her back. That was all there was to it.

"This isn't personal," he said after a moment as another tear fell. "And it's not a punishment." He softened his tone, tried to comfort her, if such a thing was possible.

It was silent for a few minutes as Sam stared out the window and he concentrated on the road. There wasn't heavy traffic, just a few cars and trucks and they were all traveling very slow.

"You said three," she said as he overtook a car. "You said there were three reasons."

He glanced at her, saw the bruised softness at her mouth, the terrible sadness in her eyes and it cut him. In the beginning, maybe he had wanted to hurt her. Maybe in the beginning he'd been driven by revenge, but he didn't know her, had thought she was one thing—a cool, impervious blonde—but that wasn't Samantha. Beneath the beautiful blond exterior was everything he'd ever wanted in a woman—warmth, tenderness, intelligence and loyalty.

"You're stunning," he said bluntly. "And I wanted you for myself."

CHAPTER SIX

HE TOOK her because he wanted her.

It was inconceivable to Sam that anyone could desire her that much. She didn't feel desirable. Didn't feel like a woman should feel.

And yet with him sitting so close, his large, powerful body crowding the car, she couldn't help but be aware of him, aware of the words he'd just spoken, and the nuances still humming in the air.

The back of Sam's neck tingled. Her stomach somersaulted. Her body felt odd all over—too sensitive, too aware. She didn't like the feeling at all, and she didn't want him to want her. She didn't want anything to do with him. Not now, not ever.

Reaching into his leather coat pocket, Cristiano retrieved his phone and after pushing a couple of buttons, handed it to her.

"Call Mrs. Bishop," he said calmly, "her number's right there. Let her know we're on our way to pick up Gabriela."

In no mood to argue, and missing Gabby, Sam dialed the number and Mrs. Bishop answered. They chatted for a moment but when Sam said they were getting close to the house to pick up Gabby, Mrs. Bishop protested. "Oh dear, that's a shame. The girls are planning a puppet show. I'm helping them with the costumes now."

Sam felt a pang. At the Rookery she'd played with the same puppets. They were Mrs. Bishop's, from her own childhood and she used to bring them to the orphanage on wet weekend afternoons so the children could play. "You're not making new costumes, are you?"

"But of course. New plays need new costumes."

Sam smiled, remembering Mrs. Bishop's needle wizardly. Mrs. Bishop was the one who'd taught Sam to cook and sew, which had been very useful skills when Sam reached the nanny college in Manchester. "Gabby must be having a ball."

"She is, Sam. She's a lovely thing and the girls are having such a good time together. Do let her stay until dinner. There's no hurry getting her home, is there?"

"Let me speak with Gabby then."

Gabby howled when she took the phone from Mrs. Bishop. "You can't pick me up now! We've made up our own play. It's our own story and we're making costumes and everything!"

"But you've been there for hours, Gabriela."

"But I don't want to go! We made cookies and had a tea party and Mrs. Bishop is helping us with the puppets. They have a puppet stage with red velvet curtains and we're going to do our play in it."

Sam glanced at Cristiano, covered the phone's mouthpiece. "Gabby wants to stay and play longer. They're going to have a puppet show."

"She's doing well, then?"

"Yes. She's having a great time."

"Then let her stay until later this afternoon. I can pick her up before dinner."

Sam told Gabby and then Mrs. Bishop what Cristiano had said, and then, call finished, Sam hung up and handed the phone back to Cristiano.

"I'm glad she's having fun. Except for school, she doesn't get to play with other children all that often," Sam said, although on the inside she felt torn. She was glad Gabby was having fun but for Sam it was awkward and uncomfortable being alone with Cristiano. "Johann wouldn't let her go to other people's houses, and her friends from school weren't allowed to come home."

"Why?" Cristiano asked.

She looked at him, and then away, and glancing out the window, Sam noticed the first snowflake fall, and then another, and another. The flakes were scattered, slow, as if indecisive about what they were going to do. "I don't know. But Gabby used to cry about it. Johann and I fought about it. It didn't matter. He never changed his mind."

"I'm sorry."

"I am, too." Maybe it was the delicate snow flurries, or the pale silver and pewter sky, but Sam felt a rush of emotion so strong she had to bite her lip to keep the tears from filling her eyes again.

She missed so much right now.

She missed virtually everything. Her parents. Charles. Even Gabby, although Gabby wasn't gone yet. "I love her," she whispered, concentrating on the view outside the car window where the snow was coming down faster and thicker now in dense white flurries. Some of the snowflakes were so big they looked like bits of lace dropping from the sky and yet they were weightless, and temperatures must have continued to drop as the snow was sticking to the ground. "Even if you take her from me, she'll always be my girl."

"Then make the transition easy on her." Cristiano's voice sounded as cold and hard as the bare limbs of the trees outside. "Help her adjust. Don't pull her in two."

It was still snowing as they reached the Rookery, and the small gamekeeper's cottage never looked smaller or darker. Sam couldn't imagine spending the rest of the afternoon alone in the dark cottage with Cristiano.

As he parked "I think I'll go to the Rookery and see if I can't locate some candles for tonight," Sam said. "The pantry used to be full of them. Every now and then we'd lose electricity and we depended on candles and kerosene lamps to get us through until the backup generator came on."

"Do you know where the lamps are?" Cristiano asked, carrying the last of the groceries into the kitchen.

"They should be in the pantry, near the candles. It's where we kept the emergency supplies."

"I'll go with you, see what we can find."

It was dark inside the Rookery. Power to the abandoned orphanage had been shut off, but once Sam got the back door open, she didn't need lights to find her way around. She'd grown up here, spent over fifteen years here. The Rookery, for better or worse, was home.

Just as she thought, she discovered boxes of candles, matches and three old kerosene lamps in the pantry off the kitchen.

"I'll take the lamps back to the cottage," Cristiano said.

Sam nodded. "I'll just have a quick look around. I'll be back soon."

With a candle to light her way, Sam walked through the Rookery's high arched hallways. The old Persian carpets were threadbare and covered only portions of the stone floor and every now and then her footsteps echoed, a too-loud clatter that bounced off the vaulted ceiling.

Nothing had changed, she thought. The furniture was all here, just a few pieces like the piano and the Georgian sofa in the parlor were covered. Everything else was exactly as she remembered. The large oil landscapes still covered the walls. The back room facing the garden was still lined with tables and chairs. That was the room they studied in, reading and writing papers and doing homework.

She'd thought the house would be dustier, dirtier, but everything was fairly tidy, and although a few cobwebs clung to the corners, it wasn't the mess she'd imagined.

Mrs. Bishop must still come in and clean, Sam thought, climbing the first of the stairs, and knowing that Mrs. Bishop still made an effort hurt more than even desertion did.

It was brighter upstairs. The windows on the second floor hadn't been boarded over and Sam's breath caught in her throat as she glimpsed the oil portrait hanging at the top of the stairs.

Reverend Charles Putnam.

Her Charles. Sam looked—his handsome face, his gentle expression, the kindness in his brown eyes—until she couldn't look any longer. He'd been her prince, her knight on a white stallion. He'd been better than she deserved.

Turning away, she pushed open one of the bedroom doors and crossed to the tall multipaned window. In this bedroom Sam could believe that time had stopped.

Nothing had changed from the night eight years ago when the world as she knew it ended and a new life began.

She'd been standing here, not far from this very window, when word had come that Charles had been killed.

She'd just begun to undress, to change from her wedding gown into her going away outfit.

Sam exhaled in a short, hard painful puff. Her fingers curled into her palms. Twice a bride, she thought, and still a virgin. But to lose Charles, the way she had…

Sam reached out to touch the windowpane. The glass was chilly, slick, a stark contrast to the lush plum velvet curtain panel, the velvet curtain the same fabric draping the bed.

God how she hated this room. And loved this room. It was Charles's bedroom, the room they were to share when they returned from their honeymoon trip to Bath.

Swallowing hard, around the thick lump filling her throat, Sam pressed her fingertips against the glass and then let her hand fall away.

Without a last look around, Sam left the bedroom, closed the door and was hurrying toward the staircase when she remembered the candle she'd left in the hall.

Sam was just returning for it when she saw Cristiano on the stairs. "Having a look around?" he asked.

She nodded, praying he didn't see the sheen of tears in her eyes. Her past was private. She didn't discuss it with anyone and she refused to give Cristiano another reason to mock her. "I'm done, though. I've seen enough."

"You haven't been to the third floor yet."

She was desperate now to get out, to escape the Rookery and its press of bittersweet memories. "I know what's up there. I used to live up there. All the children slept upstairs."

"Is it just one big room?"

"Yes, filled with dozens of beds, dozens of children who grew up without their mothers and fathers."

Back in the cottage, Sam put the kettle on the fire Cristiano had laid again this afternoon in the old cast iron stove. She stood at the kitchen window as she waited for the water to boil and watched the dense white flurries coming down. It was so quiet, so beautiful, she thought. The snow was thick and still and it covered everything in every direction.

Footsteps sounded behind, slow measured steps on the wooden floor. Sam immediately tensed, jittery all over again. Her stomach flipped. Her breasts felt tight. Goose bumps covered her skin.

She hated his effect on her.

Hated that she was so aware of him.

She didn't know why he did this to her.

She glanced over her shoulder. His arms were piled high with firewood for the stove. She had to concede he'd been quite dedicated when it came to keeping the fire burning, the wood bins filled, and the cottage warm. "Thank you."

He nodded.

"Would you like a cup of tea?" she asked, trying to cover her awkwardness.

"No. Thank you."

She turned back to the window. The snow wasn't letting up. It just continued to fall, adding to the white mounds blanketing the walls and ground outside, making the late afternoon unnaturally bright.

"It just keeps coming down," she said, all pins and needles as Cristiano arranged the wood in the bin by the stove. Her hands tightened on the edge of the farmhouse sink. Be strong, she told herself. Be confident.

"We don't get many storms like this," she continued, feeling a perverse need to fill the silence. She'd never been much of a talker, usually preferred to let her young charges chatter, but right now she felt like a high-strung child herself. "But when we do get a storm, all of England shuts down. We don't know what to do with the snow. No one's prepared, you see."

It hadn't snowed like this in Cheshire in years or she would have heard about it. And this was a true storm, the snow coming down in thick silent flurries and the snow stuck, forming dense white drifts on top of the barren window box, the bench in the garden, along the old stone wall. The whirling snow nearly obscured the great oak trees standing guard beyond the garden wall, the trees just dark hulking shadows in silent fields. It just kept falling.

He was rising, moving toward her, and he had such a leisurely way of walking, as if he had all the time in the world and there was something about his easy confidence that unnerved her even more. She'd never felt that confident about anything in life. She'd always been fearful, always afraid.

He stood next to her at the window over the sink to see what she saw. He wasn't even looking at her but she could feel him, his heat, his energy, his strength. He was so big and imposing, that it was almost as if he'd covered her world with his.

Nothing was the same since she'd met him.

Nothing about her felt the same, either.

Her emotions were all over the place. Her fears had never been stronger. She was on the edge of tears constantly but even then, she couldn't let go and cry, not really. Yet it would be such a relief to give in to the tears, such a relief to just let go of all the hurt she kept locked tightly inside of her.

But her feelings were too deep, the losses in the past too stunning, that even now, she teetered between pain and nothingness. It was as if she'd shut down somehow, somewhere, given up. Given up hope. Given up life. Given up anything that didn't have to do with Gabby.

"It was hard for you visiting the Rookery," Cristiano said now.

His observation was as unexpected as it was accurate. "Yes."

"How old were you when you were brought here?"

"Six." Just a year older than Gabby. Sam bit into her lip,

fought the wave of dark emotion, the fierce undertow of grief. She couldn't think, couldn't let herself be overwhelmed. Stay numb, she told herself, stay in control. Maybe if she hadn't lost her parents and Charles both she'd be a different person today, but she had lost them, and she couldn't change the past. She was who she was. She was what she was.

A woman who worked for others.

A woman who only lived for others.

"It doesn't look like a bad place."

"It wasn't," she whispered, hearing the catch in her voice, hating that she sounded so fragile, as if she could be easily broken. But she wasn't fragile. She'd been toughened, by time and loss. She wasn't going to break and she'd get through this. One way or another. She'd manage. She always did. That was the beauty of it. Pain didn't destroy you. It just made you stronger.

But it hurt like hell until you got to the other side.

She felt Cristiano's gaze rest on her. "How long has it been closed up?" he asked.

"Years," she answered softly, the white porcelain sink smooth beneath her fingers. "At least eight."

He wasn't even pretending to look outside anymore. He was looking at her, only at her, and the weight of his inspection made her shiver. "How long have you been widowed?"

Sam sucked in air, flinching at the pain. Talking about the Rookery was hard. Talking about Charles—impossible. Her fingers flexed convulsively against the sink's edge. "Eight," she said, looking anywhere but at him. *Eight long endless years.*

To cover her anguish, Sam turned toward the cupboard, reached for a cup and saucer. Her hand shook as she set them on the counter.

She could still feel the weight of his gaze, knew he was watching her, sensed he was remembering what Mrs. Bishop had said this morning about Sam being married and widowed in the same day, and she turned suddenly, faced him defiantly, daring him to speak about something so personal and private it still devastated her eight years later.

Her gaze clashed with his but there was no pity in his eyes, nothing in his eyes, just intense focus.

He continued to look at her with that same long, hard inspection and air bottled in her lungs. Holding her breath, she looked back at him and had never felt so vulnerable, as though she were full of holes and hurts.

Holes and hurts and broken hearts.

If only she could cry, she thought. If only she could let some of this pain out. But it was impossible. The pain was buried too deep, the loss too significant.

Inexplicably emotion flickered in Cristiano's hazel eyes. His hard jaw gentled a fraction. "You have lost a great deal in your life, haven't you?"

His sudden tenderness was too much. Sam felt a wall of ice inside her crack and fall, and behind that wall Sam glimpsed a child crying.

She didn't think she'd made a sound but Cristiano cupped her cheek, then gently sliding his hand down, over her jaw, toward her chin and across the front of her throat. "Hush," he said. "Things always work out."

Tears flooded Sam's eyes and reaching up, she caught his hand in her own and held it tightly. "You're not helping," she choked, even as her fingers curled into his. She didn't understand it. She hated his power, feared his strength, and yet somehow she craved that power and strength, too.

His head dropped and she felt his breath against her face. For a split second she thought he was going to kiss her and then the kettle whistled and he abruptly pulled back.

Sam felt his hand fall away. She took a step in the opposite direction even as she felt a shiver race through her, awareness, tension, desire.

"Your water's boiling," he said.

She turned, searched for a towel or hot pad, something to grab the kettle's handle with and when she turned around again, Cristiano was gone.

Outside Cristiano returned to chopping wood. He'd been

pouring his anger and aggression into splitting logs before he entered the cottage. He should have never stopped splitting logs. Shouldn't have carried an armful into the kitchen, not when Sam was there, not when she looked so completely and utterly alone.

He wished he hadn't seen that…that he could go back and erase her expression from his memory, the one he saw as she stood at the sink staring out the window. She'd looked so lost.

Goddamn it. She reminded him of Gabriela.

He lifted the ax, swung it high overhead and let it slam down. The impact of metal against wood shuddered through him, rippling from his arms to his shoulders and through his torso.

She wasn't alone, he told himself, yanking the blade out and turning the log, repositioning it for another swing. She was young. She was an adult. She had friends. She didn't need Gabriela. Gabriela was her job, not her life.

But, *maledizione!* The look in her eyes. The *grief.*

He swung the ax over his head again, a huge powerful arc before he brought it down, crashing into the wood. He felt a jolt through his shoulders even as the wood split and cracked. She wasn't his responsibility, he told himself, tossing the split pieces into a pile at his feet as he grabbed another large log and placed it on the chopping block. She's not my problem.

But later, as Cristiano waded through the dense snowdrifts back to the cottage, arms loaded high with freshly cut firewood, he knew she was his problem.

He'd destroyed her world, taken what little security she had away from her. At first she'd simply been a tool to get what he really wanted. But he couldn't very well leave her alone in the world—no money, no protection, no stability. If he was going to provide for Gabriela, the least he could do was provide for the one person who'd given Gabby love and affection.

Whether he liked it or not, Samantha was his responsibility, too.

He dumped the logs by the hearth in the main room, and returned outside to get one last load so they'd have enough wood for the night.

But wading back through the snow, he grit his teeth at the shooting pain in his right leg. His legs had been aching all day. At first this morning he'd thought it was the lack of sleep, but now knew it was the change of weather. Whenever there was a pressure change, his legs became hypersensitive—both skin and muscle full of stabbing pain, but he never complained, never told anyone that he hurt. He knew the dangers of his profession when he started out. He could blame no one but himself.

He swore as he hit an unanticipated patch of black ice beneath the snow. His right leg caved, nearly giving out.

Cristiano stopped, took a breath, steadied himself blocking out the searing pain. He made sure he'd found his footing before continuing on again. His rehab had covered numerous situations but walking on slick surfaces hadn't been one. But then, Monaco and the Côte d'Azur were famous for sun, not ice, so learning to cope with ice and snow had not been a priority.

Loaded down with more firewood, he turned, started back to the house and then was forced to slow, even rest, as he hit the same damn patch of ice. He had no traction in his shoes, and before his accident, ice wouldn't have been a problem, but his legs weren't the same. Nothing about his legs was the same.

The doctors had said he should always use a cane, that his weaker right leg needed the support but Cristiano was damned if he'd advertise his weakness to others. He'd never let another man know he wasn't as strong. His business was so competitive, so cutthroat, that one had to be tough—always. Not just physically, but mentally. So instead of leaning on a cane to support his weight, Cristiano had learned to compensate by walking more slowly, more deliberately. And usually it worked.

Usually.

Cristiano glowered as his right foot slipped again. Damn.

But he wasn't going to drop the wood. And he wasn't going to quit. And he wasn't going to focus on the hot sharp lancing pain that streaked through his legs now.

He'd just dumped the last load of wood by the hearth when

his phone rang. Knocking bits of bark and moss off his hands, he took the call.

It was Mrs. Bishop. She'd called to say that they'd tried to drive Gabby back but the car had slid off the road, spinning out into the field. No one was hurt but there was no way to get Gabby back, at least not with their car. As Mrs. Bishop talked, Cristiano went to the front door to check his rented Mercedes. Snow was piled a good foot high on the hood. Looking past the Mercedes he saw the entire lane was covered, no sign of road or field, fence or wall. Everything was just white, powdered white.

"I can try to drive down there," he said. "My rental car doesn't have four-wheel drive, but it might be okay."

"It might be okay," Mrs. Bishop answered anxiously, "but it might not be. Gilbert, my son-in-law, is already shaken up. Maybe it's best if Gabby just stayed here tonight, and then tomorrow we can see if one of the farmers will help us tow Gilbert's car out of the field and maybe plow the road."

Cristiano caught sight of Samantha from the corner of his eye. She must have heard the phone ring and she'd been following the conversation. "What's wrong?" she whispered. "Is Gabby all right?"

He nodded before finishing the call. "Then keep her there tonight, Mrs. Bishop, no reason to take any more risks. Tell your son-in-law I'll pay for his car to be towed, and do give us a call in the morning once everyone's up."

Hanging up, he turned to face Sam who hovered in the background. "The roads aren't drivable. Mrs. Bishop's son-in-law tried to bring Gabby home but lost control and ended up in a field or a ditch—I'm not sure which."

"Is Gabby okay?"

"Yes, but she is going to stay at the Bishops' tonight."

Sam nodded and blushed all at the same time. She'd counted on Gabby returning. But Gabby wouldn't be back tonight. Instead it would just be her and Cristiano.

Alone.

In a small cottage.

Far from neighbors.

With no electricity and no music, television or diversion.

What in God's name were they going to do for the next twelve hours?

CHAPTER SEVEN

DINNER was a simple toasted cheese sandwich served with bowls of tinned tomato soup. Not a glamorous meal but it met the need for warm food and drink.

They ate in front of the fire in the sitting room because it was the warmest spot in the cottage. Once finished, Sam stood to carry their plates and bowls to the kitchen, but as she reached for Cristiano's dishes, his eyes met hers, his gaze boring into her, the hazel-green depths warm and flecked with gold. "Leave the dishes," he said. "I'll do them later."

"That's okay. I don't mind."

"I do. Leave them."

Nervously Sam stacked the dishes in the sink before running her hands down the front of her dark gray slacks, her palms damp.

The cottage was so small. There was nowhere to go. And the bedrooms, even if she wanted to hide in there, were too cold.

But the idea of returning to Cristiano, to sitting with him near the fire filled her with dread.

He made her so jumpy. Just being near him her heart raced, her pulse pounded. She felt hot and cold at the same time, jittery, scared, uneasy.

Why was she so afraid of him?

Why did everything in her scream for her to run? Was it survival instinct? Common sense?

Glancing out the window yet again, Sam felt discouraged by

the snow still falling. "We're stuck," she said, returning to the sitting room.

Cristiano made a rough sound. "You'll survive."

Sam grimaced, sat down in one of the armchairs near the fire. "I know. Unfortunately so will you."

Cristiano surprised her by laughing, a rough deep sound that was as masculine as it was seductive. "You're really not comfortable with me, are you?"

"No!"

"Finally," he mocked, leaning back in his chair. "We get a little honesty."

"I haven't been dishonest."

He made a soft, rough sound in the back of his throat. "No. I understand. You're English, and you've cultivated through years of practice and self-denial this wonderful British stiff upper lip to keep others from knowing what you want, or need."

"That's not true. The only thing I want or need is Gabby, and I've been quite open about my feelings with regards to her."

He studied her in the red and gold firelight, his lashes lowered, his mouth firm. For a moment there was just the crackle and pop of the fire and the acrid smell of smoke. "Someday you'll marry again," he said surprisingly gentle. "You'll have children, and a family, of your own."

If he'd hoped to soothe her, his words had the opposite effect. Her throat, chest and stomach hurt as if she'd just chewed and swallowed glass. "I won't," she answered. "I'll never marry again. And I don't want children of my own."

"But you're good with children."

"I'm a nanny. My job is to look after other peoples' children. I hope I'm good with them."

"But don't you want more for yourself?"

"More, how?"

"A lover, a partner. Someone to share your life with."

She felt herself blush and she shook her head, amazed at how quickly he could fluster her. "No. I'm content." She ignored the twinge inside of her, the twinge of conscience that said she was not being entirely truthful. Truly there were times she needed more, times when she felt alone, but everyone felt lonely and alone at times. Everyone had needs. She wasn't unique that way. "My life's good."

"You've been married. How can you not miss the physical comforts? Sex? Intimacy?"

He didn't realize she didn't know anything about sex, or intimacy, and maybe that's what kept her from ever becoming more intimate with anyone. People didn't know that while on one hand she had this colorful, crazy life, on the other she was still hopelessly sheltered. Her emotions had been through hell while her body remained untouched.

Sam found it deeply embarrassing that at her age, approaching thirty, she knew as little about men and sex as she did at eighteen. Somehow a decade had come and gone and left her like one of those Dresden shepherdesses on a shelf. But she was all shattered inside.

Her mouth was so dry, her lips felt as if they were cracking. "I'm content," she repeated huskily.

"You say that, but you're not. I see it in your eyes, Samantha. I see it in the way you talk and smile. Forgive me, but you're a martyr looking for a cause."

Sam didn't realize she'd been holding her breath until her head started spinning. She forced herself to exhale and then inhale, trying to clear her head. "I'm no martyr. Some people have more heartache in their lives, some people have less."

He rose from his chair and went to the fire where he took a poker and pushed the fire around a bit before adding more fuel. "There are things I need to tell you. And I'm not sure how to tell you."

"It's bad?"

He made a rough sound. "It's not good."

Sam stiffened, not wanting more bad news. Bad news in her life had been very bad. There was no in-between news, no disappointing news, just bad as in tragic, bad as in shattering, bad as in nothing will ever be the same.

But Cristiano remained standing in front of the fire and Sam felt his gaze travel slowly over her face, his thick black lashes lowered, and yet even without seeing his expression, she felt his inspection in every muscle and every bone. "What do you have to tell me?" she begged, terrified with suspense, just wanting whatever he had to say, said, so this could be over.

"It's about Johann. I've learned things that will hurt, maybe even embarrass you. But you have to know the truth."

"Embarrass me, more than he already has?" Sam laughed mockingly. "How could he possibly embarrass me more?" She laughed again, slightly breathlessly, thinking she'd made a silly joke, and anticipating his laugh.

But Cristiano didn't smile and she suddenly felt out of breath.

"He has another wife."

Sam just stared at him. She didn't know what to do, how to react. "He *has* another wife?"

"Yes." There was no hesitation. "He still lives with her, part-time in Vienna. They were married ten years ago. He's never divorced her."

"That means…"

"Your marriage isn't valid. You're not legally van Bergen's wife."

Sam shook her head slowly. "I've never been his wife?"

"No."

"I'm not Baroness van Bergen. The wife in Vienna is."

"Yes."

She felt as though he'd taken a sledgehammer to her head and she looked up at him where he stood silhouetted by the fire, dazed. "So what am I?"

Cristiano didn't answer. He didn't have to.

Sam was nothing. Just the nanny, always just the nanny. Forever the hired help.

Sam lifted a hand, touched her forehead. "Does he have children with her?"

"No."

Thank God. "But he still sees her?"

"Yes."

"Does she know about me?"

Cristiano shook his head slightly. "I don't think so. She doesn't leave Vienna. She doesn't go out much with him."

"Neither did I." Sam laughed unsteadily. "I guess we made it convenient for him. It must be easy having two wives if you don't take out either."

"I know it's a shock, Samantha. But you're better off without him—"

"Of course I am!" She interrupted fiercely, surprised by the depth of her rage. "I didn't love him. How could I love him? He was petty and selfish, vain and self-absorbed. He was horrible to Gabriela, horrible to me, but—" And then her voice broke, and the past four years hit her and she felt devastated, betrayed. "He didn't even pay me!"

She looked up at Cristiano, alternately icy and feverish. "For three years I cooked and cleaned and sewed and gardened and received nothing. No allowance, no salary, no money, no income. Not even kindness."

She wasn't going to cry, she wouldn't cry, it was so silly. So she laughed instead and turned away, looking toward the window, hiding the fact that her eyes were burning and her heart ached. Johann had treated her abominably. And she'd let him.

Let him.

In some ways it was a relief to discover she wasn't Johann's wife, but in other ways it was mortifying. Hurtful. Shameful.

All these years she'd worked so hard. She'd scraped, scrimped, selling everything she owned to help support Johann in his decadent lifestyle. My God. He must have been laughing all the way to the bank.

"That's why he could gamble me away," she choked. "I was nothing."

"That's not true."

"It is. At least to Johann." She shook her head, not wanting sympathy, never wanting sympathy, and yet she didn't know what to do with the wretched feelings inside. "You must think me silly, but all I can think about is how he took my wedding ring back—said we needed it to pay bills. And how he insisted I cut Gabriela's hair myself since we didn't have money. And yet, he was the baron van Bergen and everyone loved him. Everyone fawned all over him while Gabby and I struggled just to get by."

"Gabby's lucky she had you, Samantha."

Her lungs burned, her eyes stung but she didn't let the tears fall. She sat up taller, straighter. "How long have you known?"

"Awhile."

"And how long is that?"

"Longer than you'd like."

She nodded jerkily. "So Johann never married Mercedes."

"They had an affair, and were still living together in Monte Carlo when Mercedes died. Johann kept Mercedes's baby."

"But *why?* Why did Johann want to adopt Gabby?"

"If I'm being generous I'll say sentimental reasons, but I'm not generous and I think his motives were purely financial. He was greedy. He thought if he adopted Gabby, he'd have access to her trust fund."

"But he wouldn't?"

"No. I'm not her guardian but I'm the trustee. Gabby doesn't even have access until she's twenty-five."

"You were right," Sam said after a moment, teeth chattering from shock not cold. "Gabby's not even five yet and already men want her for her money. It's so wrong, too. Gabby's beautiful, and smart, and funny. But even better, she has a gorgeous heart. She should be loved, and loved for herself."

"But isn't that what everyone wants?" Cristiano countered softly.

He was right. It was what she wanted, it's what she'd always wanted. She blinked back tears but Cristiano saw them. He swept the tip of his finger beneath each of her eyes to catch her tears, and she grabbed his hand, wrapped her fingers around his, and held on.

He tugged her to her feet and brought her toward him. Sam stared up into his face wide-eyed. With one hand he tilted her face to his, and the other he slid down her back, his hand so hot against her skin, his hand settling low in her back, pressing against her, melting something inside her, heating a part of her that had never been warmed.

She could feel his thighs nudge hers, feel his deep chest expand as he took a breath and then his head dropped as he cupped her face in his hand and covered her mouth with his.

As if he could feel her stiffen and resist, Cristiano gentled the kiss, stroked her cheek, her resistance melted.

Slowly he deepened the kiss, opening her mouth persuasively beneath his and Sam sighed as Cristiano's tongue slid across her tingling lower lip.

Her brain was telling her no but her body was melting into his.

And then even her brain was melting as his tongue touched hers, and his hand briefly covered her breast, his palm firm against her nipple, and she trembled, and helplessly she moved closer, wanting more, wanting him.

His kiss, and the caress, electrified her. She'd never felt anything like it. And when he eventually lifted his head, she couldn't move, couldn't think. All she could do was look at him with wide, bemused eyes.

Seeing her confusion, he smiled grimly and dropped his head, pressed another kiss to her jawbone near her ear, and whispered, "I've no morals. Don't trust me. Don't think I'm a good guy. I'm not. I will never be."

He walked out of the room, out the front door in nothing but shirt and slacks. And it wasn't him walking out that shook her, but her response to him, her response to the kiss.

She'd never felt anything like that before and it dazzled her, made her realize he was even more dangerous than she'd thought.

But it was only a kiss, she reminded herself. Cristiano had kissed many, many women in his life and Sam was sure they didn't all fall head over heels in love with him. And she wasn't head over heels in love, either.

But he had rocked her.

She'd liked the kiss, wouldn't have stopped the kiss, wouldn't have stopped him.

Her skin still tingled and tightened across her cheekbone. Her mouth felt soft, her lower lip quivering. Even her body felt warm, pliant.

She wanted him, more of him, more of whatever he could give her.

Cristiano left the cottage, stepping out into the still white landscape.

The moon was high, the snow had briefly stopped and the light shone on a distant oak tree, turning the ancient gnarled limbs into a glittering ice sculpture.

They needed to get back to Monte Carlo, he thought.

He didn't want to be here anymore. He felt increasingly trapped here. It was time to get home, get back to work, get on with his life.

Sam wasn't part of his life. He'd take care of her financially, especially since she had no money, no family, nowhere to go. He'd set her up in a little house, help her find work…

Christ, who was he kidding?

He didn't want to set her up in a little house somewhere and find her work.

He wanted to drag her into his bed and take his sweet time making love to her.

But if he took her, made love to her, kept her in his life it would ruin everything, at least complicate everything for Gabby. Because relationships ended. Love affairs didn't last forever. And then how would he explain the fallout to Gabriela?

He couldn't. She wouldn't understand. Gabby was just a child and she doted on Sam, depended on Sam, and Sam was just as devoted to Gabby.

No. Desire—attraction—stopped here. Sam was right. Gabby had to be put first. Gabby couldn't be hurt, not by the adults she trusted, not by those who'd sworn to love her, protect her.

And he did love Gabby. He loved her dearly. And he'd been

NO POSTAGE
NECESSARY
IF MAILED
IN THE
UNITED STATES

BUSINESS REPLY MAIL

FIRST-CLASS MAIL   PERMIT NO. 717-003   BUFFALO, NY

POSTAGE WILL BE PAID BY ADDRESSEE

HARLEQUIN READER SERVICE
3010 WALDEN AVE
PO BOX 1867
BUFFALO NY 14240-9952

Get FREE BOOKS and a FREE GIFT when you play the...

LAS VEGAS
GAME

Just scratch off the gold box with a coin. Then check below to see the gifts you get!

YES! I have scratched off the gold box. Please send me my **2 FREE BOOKS** and **gift for which I qualify**. I understand that I am under no obligation to purchase any books as explained on the back of this card.

▼ DETACH AND MAIL CARD TODAY! ▼

306 HDL D7YX   106 HDL D7ZY

FIRST NAME		LAST NAME

ADDRESS

APT.#	CITY

STATE/PROV.   ZIP/POSTAL CODE   (H-P-12/05)

7	7	7	Worth TWO FREE BOOKS plus a BONUS Mystery Gift!
🍒	🍒	🍒	Worth TWO FREE BOOKS!
🔔	🔔	♣	TRY AGAIN!

www.eHarlequin.com

Offer limited to one per household and not valid to current Harlequin Presents® subscribers. All orders subject to approval.

fighting for her for years, since the night of the accident when the two formula one cars slammed together in balls of red fire.

He could see it all again. It never left his mind, playing and replaying in exquisite slow motion.

And slow, slow the car came up on his right to overtake him and there, ahead of him, was his teammate's car, and Cristiano did what any aggressive ruthless driver would do. He blocked for his teammate, for his teammate's win.

But the driver on his right was even more aggressive and cut left, and then right, and somehow lost control, careening out of control.

And that was how it always began, the slow motion movie rolling in Cristiano's head, the car from the other team slamming into Cristiano's teammate and then sliding back toward Cristiano's car.

When you race, you travel at speeds beyond belief. Speed that's like flying.

There's no time to do anything. You can't prepare. Not even react.

It just happens before your eyes.

Slow, slow, a movie one never forgets.

Cristiano's teammate slams into the wall after being hit by the careening car and Cristiano, trapped by flying debris, can only go forward into his teammate's car. Into the car he'd been trying to protect, a car already in pieces.

It was his teammate—his father—one and the same.

And that's where it all ends and all begins.

The fire everywhere. Cristiano couldn't see—guided only by the smell of burning petrol and exploding flames. The only reason he survived was because God, or an angel somewhere, plucked him from the fiery inferno and willed him to live.

The first thing Cristiano knew on awakening at the hospital forty-eight hours later was that his father was dead.

The second was that his legs had been crushed and burned so badly he'd never walk again.

The third was Mercedes at the hospital weeping and screaming, *How in God's name can I have this baby now?*

Cristiano learned to walk again because a baby waited, needing a father.

He even learned to drive again because somewhere there was a baby Bartolo who'd need a strong man in his or her life, a man who wouldn't quit and wouldn't complain and would always believe that good prevailed.

Cristiano breathed deep, held the air in his chest and silently mocked himself. Don't cry, you bastard. You're a man, you can't cry.

But God, the pain. The memories. The regrets.

And to think that Gabby, who was the good, should suffer again was the worst injustice of it all. For God's sake, she'd already lost her mother, had an ass of a stepfather. How could he not do everything in his power to make Gabriela happy?

To make her life complete?

Santo Cielo, he'd do anything, absolutely anything for her.

The cottage door opened and Sam stepped out. She'd bundled up in one of the wool coats from the cottage closet. "Hey."

He nodded, features hardening, hiding all that he felt. He was so good at disguising what he felt.

"Do you mind company?" she asked, clapping her hands together and blowing on her fingers.

"You'll freeze."

"You haven't." Her blue eyes flashed up at him. "And you're not even wearing a coat."

"I'm a man."

She laughed, bless her, and he almost smiled. "That's funny?" he asked.

"Just when you say it." She glanced up, looked at the icicles above their heads, and reached up to try to break one off but couldn't. "So when are you going to tell her?" Sam asked, and her wide blue eyes, cornflower-blue, stunning blue, pierced him. "About Johann, and you and school…"

Something in her gaze set fire to his heart. And he knew about fire. He knew what it was to be burned. "That's a lot to tell a little girl," he said.

She nodded, no longer smiling, and her sober expression reminded him of the night just days ago when she'd arrived at the casino to try to convince Johann to go home.

A woman on a mission. A golden haired Joan of Arc.

"Soon," he said, shifting his weight, easing the pressure off his left leg, which had been the more severely damaged of the two. The cold weather was making all the scar tissue tight and itchy and he couldn't seem to get comfortable. "As soon as the time seems right."

"Tell me before you talk to her. Just let me know, okay?"

But he didn't say yes, and he didn't say no, he just looked at her. And as he stared into her blue eyes, his lashes drifted lower, and his gaze settled on her mouth, on the softness and fullness he'd finally kissed after waiting so long to touch, and taste. And the wait had been worth it. Her mouth was perfect. She tasted and felt divine.

Reaching out, he pushed back one of her long blond curls. "You don't hate me as much as you used to."

Even in the moonlight he could see her blush. "I never hated you," she answered, but her cheeks were crimson and she wouldn't look him in the eye.

"You didn't like me."

Fresh color swept her cheeks, and she laughed softly, and it was a surprisingly deep husky laugh for someone so slight. "I questioned your morals and values."

"That's a nice way of putting it."

"You *did* encourage Johann to gamble."

"Of course I did." He couldn't resist touching her flushed face, couldn't help touching what he'd craved for so long. "If it meant I could get what I wanted…"

"That's what made me uncomfortable. You have to have ethics, Cristiano. You can't just do whatever you want because you want something."

Now it was his turn to laugh. "Oh, yes, you can," he said, pushing the door open and steering her back in.

CHAPTER EIGHT

AFTER the kiss, Sam was sure that something would happen, but after returning to the fire, Cristiano lost himself in some reading he'd brought with him and Sam sat in her chair, feeling nervous and excited, rather like a girl going to her first dance.

But nothing else happened. It was as if the kiss had never occurred.

Cristiano focused on his reading and Sam sat feeling like a wallflower.

He must regret kissing me, she thought, chewing on her thumb. Or he kisses so many women it's really nothing.

She had a sneaking suspicion it was the latter.

Finally it was time for bed, and Cristiano slept in one of the bedrooms while Sam carried blankets to the couch in the sitting room.

It took her forever to fall asleep and when she woke up stiff and cold in the morning, her mood was not much better.

Her mood didn't improve later, either, when during breakfast she felt him watching her.

Sam did her best to ignore him, just like she struggled to ignore the buzzy butterflies in her middle. He doesn't even remember the kiss, she told herself sternly. You can't dwell on it, either.

But it was hard to forget, especially after such a sleepless night where she lay awake for hours, thoughts tormented, body hot, and empty, craving satisfaction.

Breakfast over, Sam attacked the few dishes, scrubbing the plates that had nothing more than crumbs on them. Cristiano came up behind her to set his cup on the counter and she jumped as if somebody had touched her with a hot wire.

Just the knowledge that he was near her, behind her, made her acutely sensitive. And when he leaned past her, to pick up a dish towel and dry the dishes she'd washed, she felt a coil in her middle that actually hurt.

If this was desire it was awful.

It wasn't fun. It was fierce. Hot. *Angry.*

She felt maddened by it, by want, by the unknown.

She must have sighed or made some sound because Cristiano looked down at her, one black eyebrow lifting. "Something bothering you today?"

She tossed the scrub brush down, faced him, one hand gripping the sink. *"Yes."*

His hazel gaze slowly traveled the length of her, resting provocatively on her throat, her breasts, her hips. "Tell me what it is. Maybe I can help."

"You can't help. You're the problem."

"I'm the problem?"

She shook her head in exasperation. Why did she say that? It was dumb to say that. No, he wasn't the problem. She was the problem. This—the attraction, the situation—it was her problem. She couldn't handle her feelings, or her response. He'd kissed her—big deal—but God help her, she wanted more.

And the intensity of her feelings made her feel like an ignorant schoolgirl. She'd loved the kiss. But she wasn't a schoolgirl. She was a spinster. A spinster leveled by a kiss.

"You haven't told me why I'm the problem," he said.

Sam glanced out the window toward the driveway as if Gabby would just magically appear and save her from this. "Ignore me. I'm being irrational."

"You're the least irrational woman I've ever known. Tell me. Let me try to help."

Then that would require kissing me again, she thought, looking up at him, into the hard angles of his face and eyes that held her, mesmerized her. "Please don't be charming," she whispered, only half-jesting. "I don't think I can handle it. Not from you, not today, not after last night."

"What about last night?"

So he didn't even remember. The kiss hadn't meant anything, or made an impression.

Sam whimpered, she hadn't meant to, she couldn't keep the hurt in.

But suddenly he was closer, or she was closer, and the heat between them was scorching. Sam felt hot, her clothes too tight and suddenly she couldn't breathe anymore.

And then he was reaching for her, his arms wrapping around her, pulling her against him creating a riot of sensation. Just that one touch of his body against hers and it was like New Year's and fireworks, sparks exploding everywhere. She felt him everywhere, too—chest, ribs, hips, thighs. He was hard, strong, male, and it was the most delicious feeling in the world, her body alive, her body aware of his, her body feeling warm and real and good.

His hand was in the small of her back, urging her even closer and she felt the throb of him against her, his body's heat and how his body strained.

She'd thought when it came to this, she'd be afraid. She'd thought if a man ever held her so close, teased her with his body like this, made her aware of his desire, she'd thought she'd panic. Hate it. Run.

Instead she wanted to slide her hands beneath his shirt, feel the warmth of his skin beneath her palms, reach for his waistband and let the clothes fall away.

And then she did reach for his belt and waistband, fumbled with the clasp, gave up to touch his flat abdomen and the warm firm muscle banding his ribs.

His hands were against her hips, shaping her, caressing her, and it seemed like the most natural thing in the world to have him touch her.

I think I could love him, she thought, wrapping one arm around his neck, standing on tiptoe. I think I could love him. And maybe it was only lust, but it felt right and honest and for the first time in years she felt right, too.

She'd finally given in to need, to want, to hunger. She'd finally admitted she craved touch, love, pleasure. And as Cristiano stroked down the outside of her thigh, and then up the inside, his fingers between her legs, touching her where she was most sensitive, she knew that in this respect at least, Cristiano had been made for her.

He was the right man to take her virginity.

He was the right man to teach her about making love.

A loud horn sounded outside, not a normal car horn but a beeping blaring sound that jolted Sam and Cristiano apart. They jumped and looking up they saw the yellow tractor and Gabriela bundled in borrowed winter clothes, jumping down.

Gabby was back and for the first time ever, Sam wished the little girl could have stayed away another hour.

Gabby came bursting into the house, laughing and breathless while the white-haired farmer climbed off his tractor to follow Gabriela.

Sam and Cristiano met the farmer on the doorstep. "We got you your girl back," the farmer said, cheeks ruddy with cold. "Later today we'll try to get your driveway plowed."

"When you've time," Cristiano said, thanking the farmer and sliding a folded bill into his hand.

The farmer nodded, pocketed the twenty-pound note and turned away before turning back. "She told me you're Cristiano Bartolo," the farmer said, indicating Gabby. "And I wondered if maybe you're not Bartolo's boy. You sure look like him. Italian, and all."

Cristiano smiled. "I am."

"Well, I'll be." The farmer clapped Cristiano on the shoulder once. "You're a good man. I like you." He nodded at Sam, chucked Gabriela under the chin and headed back to his tractor.

But before Sam could organize her thoughts, before she could ask Cristiano what the farmer had meant, Gabriela was dancing around them. "It's like a fairyland outside," she cried, jumping from one foot to the other. "Come see, Sam. It's like *The Nutcracker* ballet. It's magic!"

It was indeed magic, Sam had to agree, standing with Gabby at the open cottage door.

The great oak trees were covered in white. Icicles glistened from the edge of the cottage roof. Bright powdery snow glittered beneath bright blue skies and sunlight that had never been clearer or more golden.

"Let's go for a walk," Gabby cried, still bundled in her borrowed winter clothes.

Actually a walk sounded exactly like what Sam needed and she went to get her coat while Gabby waited out front.

Gabby looked like a puffy blue marshmallow as she smiled up at Cristiano. "Are you coming with us?"

"For a walk?" he asked.

"Yes."

He shook his head. "No. I'll skip the exercise."

"Exercise is good for you," Sam said, sliding her arms into her coat. She didn't have the warm clothes Gabby did but a brisk walk should help warm her up.

"So is a toasty fire," he answered dryly.

Sam made a face at him then extended a hand to Gabriela. "Suit yourself. We'll be back in a little bit."

Outside, the air was biting cold and the snow deep and powdery. They set off for the Rookery, but walked around the back of the old building to what had once been the kitchen garden.

Almost immediately they sank knee deep into a chilly white mound. Gabby gasped even as Samantha did.

"It's freezing," Gabriela said breathlessly.

"Look," Sam said, pointing to the edge of the roof where melting snow had frozen into long spinning strands of ice. "Isn't that the most gorgeous icicle? Looks like a waterfall."

"Like in Switzerland," Gabby agreed, as they tramped further on, slow quiet steps that required lots of concentration on Gabby's part.

Sam glanced down at the top of Gabby's head. "You remember that trip?"

Gabby's fingers tightened. "We went for a ride in a carriage and had bread in melted cheese for supper."

Gabby wasn't even three yet then. "That was two years ago."

Gabby's hazel eyes narrowed. "It was fun."

Sam's chest squeezed with emotion. "It was fun," she agreed softly. The visit to Bern had been the first—and last—trip Sam had taken with Gabby and Johann. Johann had said he had business in the city and while he attended meetings, Sam and Gabby played tourist, taking a horse-drawn carriage through the city and then stopping later on the way back at a chalet-style restaurant where they sat outside beneath a heat lamp and dunked chunks of crusty bread in a golden cheese fondue.

They were hurting a little as they reached the back garden where dormant rosebushes looked like snow-flecked sculptures.

Sam brushed snow off one of the benches and she and Gabby sat. Almost immediately Sam could feel the chill from the bench seep through her pants.

"Has he come to take me back with him?" Gabby asked, touching Sam's sleeve.

Sam covered Gabby's mitten with her gloved hand. For a moment she couldn't bring herself to speak, not trusting her voice.

"I heard him," Gabby added. "That first night he was here when you thought I was sleeping."

Sam tried to sound severe. "You shouldn't eavesdrop. Because the problem with eavesdropping," she added more gently, "is that you don't always hear the whole conversation and you miss the meaning of what is being said."

"So he's not going to take me home?"

Sam lifted Gabby's mitten hand, pressed a kiss to her fuzzy palm. "Not without me, he isn't."

Cristiano stood at the kitchen window watching Samantha and Gabriela make their way back to the cottage. They made a picture, he thought, teeth scraping as he bit back the hot emotion rushing through him.

Fair, pink-cheeked Samantha, her long loose spiral curls dusted with snow, bent down to hear whatever it was Gabriela was saying, and Sam looked exactly the way he imagined a snow angel would look. And Gabriela, with her long dark hair escaping her cap in wisps, black tendrils clinging to her cheeks that were rosy from the cold, looked so vibrantly alive that it made Cristiano's heart hurt.

Gabby should always look so healthy and happy.

He'd do everything in his power to ensure her health and happiness.

As he watched, Sam impulsively wrapped her arm around Gabby's shoulders, giving her an affectionate squeeze and he smiled reluctantly. Sam and Gabby looked nothing alike and yet they suited each other perfectly. And Sam, even though she'd been employed as Gabby's nanny, was more mother than any mother he'd ever seen.

He left the doorway, went to the fireplace in the living room, held his hands over the heat.

It was difficult being here with them when they were together. They had such a long history together and even though he was Gabby's family, he felt like the outsider.

He was the outsider. And that hurt.

The front door opened and voices and light filled the cottage. Cristiano blinked at the brightness of the light and yet welcomed the warmth they brought to the cottage. Sam and Gabriela literally lit up a room.

"Cristiano," Gabby called from the doorway, still wheezing from laughing and running in the snow. "Come play with us."

Play in the snow? Cristiano grimaced. Maybe as a child he'd loved to ski, but since his accident, he avoided snow and ice. "How about a card game instead?" he suggested.

Gabby appeared in the living room, cheeks red, light hazel eyes fringed by long black lashes. She clapped her gloved hands sending little snow flurries across the room. "But it's beautiful outside!"

"And cold."

"*Pssh,*" she said dismissively, waving one gloved hand in his direction. "You're not that old. Come out and play. It'll be fun. It's snow."

He wasn't that old.

Bene, grazie, he thought. Great, thanks. And yet he was amused. Women chased him. He was never short of female company, most adored his wealth, his looks, his celebrity status, and yet here he was, sequestered with two who seemed impervious to his charms.

And then as Cristiano looked down into Gabby's little face, her dark eyes so much like his, his heart ached. "I don't play in snow very well," he said gruffly.

"That's okay. All you have to do is try your best."

What a minx. She was certainly her father's daughter. "Is that all?" he drawled, mocking her.

"Yes." She reached for his hand, tugged on it, leading him toward the door. "Do you need your coat? It's chilly out."

It was as if she'd taken his heart in her small fingers, instead of his big calloused hand. He bit down on the inside of his cheek to hide the intense emotions filling him. He'd spent his life wanting family, craving a traditional family, but it had never been his to have. His father wasn't the sort to settle down. His father wasn't the sort to want anything but speed. Risk. Danger. Cristiano had it in his blood, too, but not to the extent his father did.

And Gabriela…

Cristiano shook his head, amazed by her bright eyes, quick mind, unflinching nature. He knew he'd never actually send her to boarding school, especially not after the miserable experiences he'd had. But Samantha didn't have to know that. Let Sam think he was a brute. Let her think the worst. He didn't need her approval, and he didn't need her to like him. He just needed Gabriela to come home.

Sam blew on her fingers as Gabby led Cristiano out of the house by the hand. He, like Sam, didn't have warm winter

clothes, and she supposed she could have dug through the closets and bureau drawers at the Rookery to find heavier coats and
caps and gloves, but it seemed wrong. The Rookery had been
shut up so long, closed after Charles died, it felt more like a
shrine to Charles than a place orphan children had once lived.

But Cristiano, even gloveless, tackled the snowman with
Gabby, helping pack big snowballs and then stack the balls to
form the snowman's body. Together they hunted up sticks for
arms and ransacked the kitchen for a carrot for the nose, but sadly
all the carrots were used in the shepherd's pie, but they finished
with stones for the eyes and mouth and then Gabby's cap and
scarf.

Sam was just about to warm milk for hot cocoa when
Cristiano and Gabby returned. They were laughing, shivering
and discussing the merits of their snowman they'd named most
originally, Mr. White.

"Let's get out of your wet clothes," Sam said, taking Gabby's
cold, damp hand in hers. "I think you'll need a warm bath, too.
You're frozen through."

"But it was fun!" Gabby cried, turning to look at Cristiano
for affirmation. "Wasn't it?"

He nodded, and his thick dark hair, worn long, formed inky
ringlets on his brow. The curls hadn't been so prominent earlier
and Samantha suspected that tramping about in the snow had
brought the curls to life.

And Gabby smiled broader, dimpling with pleasure. She
couldn't look away from Cristiano, her gaze riveted to his face.

He was very handsome, Sam admitted silently, reluctantly.
With the chiseled features, the very strong nose, and dark lashed
eyes, Cristiano was good-looking in that hunky Italian film star
way, but Sam knew that's not why Gabriela adored him.

Gabriela adored him because he talked to her, listened to her,
made her feel important. And with a pang Sam realized Gabby
had never had this before, not from a man anyhow.

Johann had spent very little time with Gabby, and the time
they did spend together inevitably revolved around Johann's

mood, Johann's temper, Johann's problems. Tragically Gabby had been lost in the shuffle and it was only now that Sam began to understand how much the little girl had craved attention, and needed love, from a father. Gabby might have called Johann Papa, but Johann had never been her father. Not in name, not in word, not in deed.

"You're not leaving now, are you?" Gabby asked him, as Sam tugged on her hand, trying to steer her toward the small bathroom.

For a moment Cristiano said nothing and then he shook his head slowly. "No." His voice was sober. "I'm not going anywhere without you."

Gabby's smile returned, and it was bright, all light and happiness. "Good. And we'll take Sam with us when we go."

We'll take Sam with us when we go.

Gabby's innocent words echoed in Sam's head while Sam prepared the makeshift bath. Sam had essentially said the same thing to Gabby on their walk earlier in the afternoon, but it was different coming from Gabby.

Once Gabby was out of the bath and dry, Sam dressed her and towel-dried her hair, and let her sit close to the fire while Sam combed her wet hair. "I'll bring your cocoa in here," she said to Gabby. "Don't sit too close to the fire, though. I'll be right back."

And even though Sam wasn't gone more than a couple minutes, by the time she'd returned with the cup of hot chocolate, Gabriela was out, sound asleep in front of the fire, a fistful of old tin soldiers in her hand.

Sam covered Gabby with a blanket and went to hang up the towels and wet winter clothes to dry. Cristiano was still in the bathroom so Sam headed into his room first but on opening the door she discovered she'd been mistaken.

Cristiano wasn't in the bathroom anymore. He'd already finished his bath and she'd caught him with his back turned toward her just starting to dress. Sam stopped short at the sight of a naked Cristiano. His back was broad and tan, his hips narrow, his buttocks muscular, hard, but paler than his back and legs. But it was his thighs that caught her attention. His thighs, though thickly muscled, were heavily scarred.

Burns, she thought. Burns and more. A long incision indicating he'd been cut. Surgery, yes. But whether for setting broken bones or a skin graft, she didn't know.

Cristiano had heard the door open and he turned suddenly, covering his lower belly with his towel. "Thank God you're not Gabby."

She made a soft incoherent sound. His chest was as tan and muscular as his back, his biceps knotted with muscle but the front of his thighs were like the back—scarred, disfigured with scars that ran down his hard, carved quadriceps toward his knees.

He saw she was staring and she flushed, looked away and then up into his face. His gaze met hers, and he gave her a long level look but said nothing.

"I was going to dry Gabby's wet things in here," she said awkwardly. "They're still so wet."

"Leave them on the bed. I'll do it."

She nodded, a hasty embarrassed nod, before dropping the clothes and leaving.

But back in the living room Sam couldn't forget what she'd seen. Cristiano's skin, so tan and gorgeous above his hips, looked nothing short of tortured below. He'd obviously been badly hurt, burned in a fire. But how and when?

Cristiano reappeared moments later, dressed, his black hair combed, the curls tamed, the sage linen shirt open at the throat, the tails out over his sturdy khaki pants. He was so tall, so male that Sam found herself wanting to move toward him, to touch him and see if he was as warm and hard as he looked.

It was a crazy thought. It made no sense because she didn't trust him, didn't want to like him, and yet she was also so drawn to him, like a fly to sticky paper.

Her attraction, as well as her ambivalence, scared her. She hadn't been attracted to a man in years and years…since Charles, actually, and yet as much as she cared about Charles, she'd never felt this kind of curiosity or interest. She'd never really thought of Charles as a man. In her mind, Charles was always just a good person—kind, compassionate, saintly—but not physical, and certainly not sexual.

"When did she fall asleep?" Cristiano asked, gesturing to Gabriela who was curled up on the floor.

"Right after her bath. I went to get her hot cocoa, and when I came back she was out."

"I worry about her sleeping so close to the fire. I'll carry her to bed." Cristiano crouched down and scooped Gabriela into his arms as though she weighed nothing, and yet as he stood, she saw his jaw tighten, an almost imperceptible tensing of the muscles in his jaw.

He still hurt, she thought.

Funny, if she hadn't seen the actual burns on his thighs, she wouldn't have known he'd been injured. He compensated well, but now she could see things she hadn't seen before, the adaptations he'd made to compensate for loss of agility, probably even muscle weakness. Like his slower walk. She'd thought it was arrogance, confidence. Instead it was practicality. And when he sat, he nearly always chose a chair with arms, sitting down by leaning on the chair's right arm, and then dropping into the seat.

As he returned to the living room she studied his walk more closely, saw for the first time the slight hitch in his step, how he put a little more weight on one leg than the other.

Probably playing with Gabby in the snow hadn't helped, she thought. He didn't have boots and in his leather dress shoes he wouldn't have had much traction.

He casually took a seat in one of the old leather chairs facing the fire. And he did just what she remembered: he leaned on the chair's right arm, dropped his right hip onto the leather cushion and then the left. His thick hair, now nearly dry, looked glossy in the firelight and the dark beard shadowing his jaw emphasized his straight nose and his firm expressive mouth.

And Sam, who'd felt such conflicting, ambivalent things for Cristiano, felt something new. Tenderness. Admiration.

Despite everything, she liked him. But she had no desire to

complicate an already complicated situation, so any attraction she felt would have to be suppressed. Gabriela came first. Gabriela's stability was everything.

"I'm sorry I walked in on you," Sam said, taking a seat on the couch. "I should have at least knocked."

"It's fine. I'm sure it's not the first time you saw a naked man."

She nodded, blushing a little, thinking there was no point in telling him that she actually hadn't seen that many naked men. He probably wouldn't believe that she was still a virgin at twenty-eight.

She waited a moment, hoping he'd say something about the burns she'd seen, but he didn't, and it really wasn't any of her business.

If change was required, it was on Sam's part. Sam knew she was too sensitive, too shut-down, too controlling. She'd thought it was her nanny training, but it wasn't the two years spent at nanny college that had made her so disciplined. It was fear.

Sam was afraid of life. Afraid of death. Afraid of everything in between.

"I don't even know what you do," she said breathlessly, trying to regain some sense of control. "Who *are* you?"

Grooves formed on either side of his mouth as he fought his smile. "Cristiano Bartolo—"

"Yes. I know your name. But *who* are you? Why do people know you? And people do know you—that night at dinner in Monte Carlo—people approached you. Gave you their blessings. Even Johann thought I should know you. What do you do?"

His head tipped, thick lashes dropping, before he looked up at her. "I'm a Formula 1 driver."

He said it simply, no arrogance in his voice or answer. In fact, his voice was expressionless but he was watching her closely. "Do you know what that is?"

"You race cars."

Sam suddenly wished she hadn't asked the question. "Isn't that terribly dangerous?"

She could have sworn he smiled but then the smile was gone

and his features were so hard he looked like someone else altogether. "Can be," he said coolly.

When he didn't elaborate, Sam realized that was all he was going to say.

CHAPTER NINE

"I'M GOING to tell her." Cristiano said the next morning while Sam boiled water for tea and Gabby sat on the floor near the fire making snowflakes from paper Cristiano had in his briefcase. "She should know the truth."

Sam glanced uncertainly at him. "I agree…"

"But?"

So he'd heard the reservation in her voice. Sam rearranged the cups and saucers on the counter. "But she's only just lost her father."

"He wasn't her father."

"She thinks he is."

"That's why she should know the truth."

"Don't you think it's just a lot for her to take in? Out with the old house, the old school and the old father and in with the new?"

He gave her a hard look. "I won't tell her about school yet."

"That's good."

He leaned close to Sam, so close that her middle filled with heat and her lower belly grew tight and even her breasts felt strange, the bra chafing her now very sensitive nipples. "Your sarcasm isn't helping," he said.

She swallowed hard. "I don't want her upset."

"It's natural for her to be upset. What's happened is upsetting. But the good news is that I'm not going away. I've found her, I have her, and she'll always have me."

Sam suddenly resented him for making so much sense. *She'd* been the one trained at Princess Christian College in Manchester. She'd been the one that wore the sturdy brown uniform for two years. She'd been the one who'd undergone rigorous training in how to cope with difficult situations and all kinds of children.

The kettle whistled and Sam grabbed a pot holder and moved it off the heat. "When will you tell her then?" she asked, just able to see far enough into the living room where she caught the motion of Gabby folding the paper again and then snipping, and then folding once more, and snipping.

"Now," he answered.

And suddenly Gabby's life looked as delicate as the paper snowflake she was making. Fragile. Ethereal. "Oh, Cristiano, can't we wait a little longer—"

But he didn't let her finish the thought. He walked out of the kitchen into the living room and crouched next to where she was still fashioning her snowflake. "Gabby, if the roads are clear enough later, we're going back to Monaco today."

Gabby set the paper and scissors down. "Do you think the roads will be cleared?"

"I'm hoping."

She nodded. "Me, too. I miss the sun."

Cristiano's expression suddenly eased. "I feel the same way." He crouched next to Gabby. "But when we go back, you're not going home to your old house. You'll be coming to live with me—"

"And Sam?" Gabby interrupted, looking at Sam where she stood in the doorway.

"I'm going, too," Sam said, gently reassuring.

"Oh, good."

"And are you going to get married?" Gabby asked.

Sam blanched, hastily shook her head. "*No.* No. Cristiano and I are just friends."

"But you *will* get married, right?" Gabby persisted.

"No, Gabby." Sam's tone sharpened even as her body prickled with heat. This was getting really uncomfortable. "We're going back to Monaco so you can return to school and we're going to take care of some business. But there's no wedding."

Gabby frowned grumpily. "Why not? I like Cristiano better than Papa."

"About that," Sam said after a brief, and very awkward silence, "there's something we need to tell you. Something about your father."

"I know what it is," Gabby answered.

"Um, no Gabriela, I don't think you do."

The girl sighed, leaned back in her chair, her small features set in lines of exasperation. "Papa's not my real father."

Sam nearly lost her balance. She put out a hand, braced herself on the door frame. "You *know?*"

Gabby smiled but the smile didn't reach her eyes and for a moment she looked very small, and very young, every bit the vulnerable five-year-old. "I used to have a baby book. My mommy made it for me. But Papa Johann took it away." Gabby hesitated and rare tears shone in her eyes. "The book said my real papa's name is Enzo Bartolo. He's a race car driver like Cristiano. But I never met him."

If it were any other child, Sam would say this was a fit of imagination. Children as young as Gabriela couldn't possibly keep facts straight, but Gabby had a mind and memory that was unlike any child's she'd ever known.

But even suspending disbelief, Sam didn't know what to say, or how to comfort Gabriela. The conversation had taken dramatic turns, sharp right, steep left, and now there was only silence and the sound of Gabriela breathing heavily.

Then Cristiano cleared his throat. "I met him, Gabby," he said quietly. "I knew him."

Gabby looked up at him, eyes bright with tears, touchingly hopeful. "You did?"

He nodded, picked up Gabby's hand and kissed it. "I think you would have liked him a lot, Gabby. He was my father, too."

The secrets, Sam thought later as they traveled to Manchester, the secrets and shadows each person kept buried inside…

It boggled her mind, the facts, the truth, the way things were.

Cristiano wasn't Gabby's father. He was her half-brother. Mercedes wasn't Cristiano's lover, but his father's, Enzo's, girl-friend. Enzo had never come forward to claim his daughter be-cause he died, just months before Gabriela was born.

Sam closed her eyes, drew her arm even more closely around Gabriela who slept curled in her lap during the flight from Manchester back to Nice on Cristiano's private jet.

Life was a series of events, cause and effect. One thing led to another, to another, and another. And as unbearable as it sounded, it also made sense.

Pregnant, alone and grieving, Mercedes ended up with Johann.

Did Enzo know he was going to be a father again before he died? Did Johann always know who Gabby's real father was? Did Gabby remember her mother at all?

Sam opened her eyes at the sound of footsteps on the dense mushroom colored carpet. The jet had been furnished in shades of taupe and gray and Cristiano took a seat in one of the soft gray leather chairs opposite the leather sofa where Sam sat with Gabriela.

"We're almost there," he said, with a glance toward the window. "My driver's waiting. We just need to decide where we want to go. My penthouse in Monte Carlo, or the villa in Cap Ferrat. It's your decision."

"I don't know either."

"One is a city apartment, and the other is my home on the peninsula."

"Where do you think Gabby would like best?" Sam asked.

"The villa. It's near the beach."

They lapsed into silence as the flight attendant on board the jet approached to let them know that they'd soon begin their descent.

"Cristiano," Sam said, as the flight attendant walked away. "What happened…and again yesterday…" She took a quick breath, needing to say what she needed to say before they landed and Gabriela woke. "That wasn't anything, was it?"

"What?"

"The, um, kiss."

Cristiano's upper lip curled. His expression hardened, turned mocking. "You're bothered by it?"

"I—" She took a quick breath. "I just wasn't sure what you meant by it, or if you meant nothing. I'm sure you meant nothing. It was just a kiss."

She'd been trying to reassure herself, trying to let him know it was okay but somehow she was saying the wrong words. She could tell from his expression that every word that came from her mouth just made him angrier, more irritated. She'd somehow struck a nerve, and hadn't even meant to.

"What I meant was that I'm sorry I…" Her voice faded away and she bit her lip, tried again. "Sorry I…"

"Kissed me back?"

She blushed, miserable. "I know it shouldn't have happened. I wasn't thinking. I suppose I was scared, overwhelmed. Maybe I needed comfort." She exhaled, wondered where she'd gone wrong, how a simple apology had gotten so convoluted. "So I'm sorry."

"For what? Needing comfort? Or enjoying the kiss?"

My God this was hard, almost impossible. She was an adult, a woman, and she couldn't even calmly discuss a kiss. "I don't have your experience and I'm certain you kiss women all the time, and it's nothing, I know kissing means nothing to you—"

"I only kiss women I like. Women I'm attracted to." His lips curved, his expression sardonic. "Women I'd like to sleep with. So don't apologize. I wanted you, wanted to bed you. It just wasn't convenient."

Then he stood, went to the table where he'd been working during most of the flight and sat down again to finish the paperwork he'd started earlier.

Stomach churning, Sam watched him resume reading even as the plane started its steep final descent. Ever since she met him, life hadn't been the same.

On the ground in Nice, Cristiano's chauffeur was waiting for them. The driver greeted them at the executive terminal, loaded their luggage into the car and then they were off, heading to Cristiano's villa on the Cap Ferrat peninsula.

Of course Sam knew that the peninsula was considered a playground for the rich. You couldn't drive along the coast without being confronted by the lavish villas, fabulous gardens and extravagant yachts moored in the St-Jean marina, but she'd never been included in the parties, or inside any of the villas. She might have married Baron van Bergen three and a half years earlier, and he might have attended events, but she'd never been on the guest list.

Sam felt a wiggle at her side and glancing down saw that Gabriela was trying to sit higher in her seat to get a better look out the window. "I can't see the houses!" Gabby complained. "There are too many fences and bushes in the way."

Gates and hedges, not fences and bushes, Sam silently corrected as she ruffled Gabby's hair. "You're so excited," she teased. "You'd think you'd never been anywhere."

"I haven't been *here*."

Here being Cristiano's home, and they'd arrived, the car slowing, stopping as the gates slowly opened, revealing little by little an exquisite villa tucked discreetly behind the tall dark green hedges that Gabby deplored.

And yet once they'd passed through the ornate wrought-iron gates, they glimpsed the startling blue ocean and then the Belle Epoque villa that nestled jewel-like in mature gardens marked by fanciful topiaries, verdant lawns, and flowers spilling from vines, pots, and fragrant, vibrant beds.

The car had barely stopped before Gabby was scrambling out, delighted by the endless lawn and the breathtaking view of the St-Jean marina where great white yachts dotted the blue and turquoise water.

Cristiano followed Gabby as she ran toward the stone wall of the terraced garden. "The pool!" she cried, turning around and gesturing excitedly. "Sam, there's a pool here, too."

Sam followed more slowly, smelling orange blossoms and

pine in the breeze that caught at her hair. Tucking a strand of hair behind her ear, Sam wrapped her thin lettuce-green cardigan closer to her body, hugging herself. She wasn't cold, just overwhelmed.

In the car during the drive Cristiano had rattled off some of the names of his neighbors and she'd been amazed, but never in her wildest dreams had she imagined anything like this.

It wasn't just that Cristiano's villa looked like a delicious marzipan confection, or that the lush gardens rivaled anything she'd ever seen anywhere, it was the view. She'd lived for years in the Côte d'Azur, enjoyed the sunshine, admired the pretty beaches but the view took her breath away. As you drove along the coast, you could see beaches and marinas, villas cut into the terraced mountain, quaint red-tiled roofs in charming fishing villages, but here at Cristiano's home on the Cap, you could see it all, together, in one picture postcard view.

The green land curved around the azure sea, creamy stone buildings clustered at the water's edge, their beige and pink stone topped by red clay tiles while narrow stone piers and walls provided protected beaches and shelter for yachts and fishing boats.

Cristiano turned, smiled a welcome at Sam as she reached them.

"How could you live anywhere else?" she asked, arms still wrapped tightly around her middle. She felt like a little girl presented with the prettiest bride doll ever. She could only look. Couldn't bear to touch. It couldn't be real.

He shrugged. "Monte Carlo's close, convenient. It's where the corporate offices for The Bartolo Driving School are and that's where I spend most of my time these days."

"So that's what you do now?"

"I'm proud of the company. We're an international racing school now with campuses and tracks in the United States, Brazil, and Italy of course. But we don't just train for road racing, we've really moved into executive protection and antikidnapping courses where we work with corporations, executives, their families and staff teaching them to detect and deter potential vehicular confrontations and assault."

Sam looked at him, intrigued, thinking of the kidnapping attempt at Gabby years ago. "And these are classes?"

"Four and seven day courses, and they're popular. Our schools have wait lists for them right now. Think about it, nearly everyone would benefit from specialized training in maximum car control. While most people won't ever need to know counterterrorist tactics, it'd never hurt to have more confidence behind the wheel."

Gabby suddenly turned around. "Can I try?" She asked, pushing long dark hair from her face since she'd lost her hairband somewhere since leaving the plane. "I'd like to drive fast."

"You mean drive safe," Sam corrected.

Gabby grinned so hard her nose wrinkled. "No, fast. I want to go fast. I want to drive race cars, too."

Cristiano smiled but Sam wasn't amused. She shot Cristiano a sharp look. "This is your doing," she reproached.

"She's a Bartolo," he answered, scooping Gabby into his arms. "It's in her blood."

Gabby wrapped an arm around his neck and took a deep breath. "I like it here. I like it very much." She looked out over the blue and green vista before glancing at Sam. "I think you and Cristiano should get married and then we can all live here and be happy forever."

Sam heard the hint of wistfulness in Gabby's voice and it tugged on Sam's heart. Gabby had never had a real family, and more than anything, Sam wanted that normalcy for Gabby. But marrying Cristiano wouldn't make them a normal family. Sam had learned the hard way that marriages of convenience were marriages of inconvenience. They didn't work.

"Let's see about lunch," Cristiano said, shifting Gabby in his arms. "I know the cook was planning something special."

Gabby leaned toward Cristiano, cupped her hand around her mouth and whispered in his ear.

Sam had no idea what Gabby said but Cristiano began to laugh, a deep belly laugh that rumbled out of him. As he laughed, Gabby giggled, too and turning toward Sam, Cristiano shot her an apologetic smile. "Gabby just hopes it's not Mrs. Bishop's famous shepherd's pie."

After lunch, one of the young women Cristiano employed took Gabby down to the heated outdoor pool for a swim. Sam expressed concern about letting Gabby go swimming with a virtual stranger and Cristiano explained that nineteen-year-old Marcelle worked at one of the local hotel pools as a lifeguard during the summer. "Marcelle teaches many of the local children to swim, and I've known her and her family for years. Gabby's safe, I promise."

It wasn't until Gabby had gone skipping out of the villa in her suit and terry-cloth cover-up with swim goggles in hand that Sam acknowledged her true fear—being alone with Cristiano.

The kiss yesterday afternoon was never far from her mind.

If it had been a bad kiss, or a sweet kiss, something she could easily dismiss she'd feel different about being alone with Cristiano, but the kiss hadn't been bad, and it was far from sweet.

Sam buttoned the bottom of her delicate green cardigan. "Is there something I can do to help Gabby settle in? Laundry? Prepare her room? Unpack?"

"I have people who do laundry and clean. That's not your job anymore."

"Then what is my job?" she answered, feeling completely at a loss. Growing up she'd thought the Rookery was the most beautiful place she'd ever seen. It had seemed like a castle with its thick paned windows, beamed ceilings, narrow stairwells and secret passageways. But Cristiano's villa was a palace. Indeed, it'd been built in the late nineteenth century, not long after King Leopold II of Belgium's Les Cedres, and Beatrice Ephrussi de Rothschild's Villa Ile-de-France.

"To come sit and talk with me. Relax a little."

She buttoned another two buttons. "I'm not sure sitting with you would be relaxing."

He looked at her and his lips curved, his expression knowing. He was confident, very confident, and that unnerved her even more. This was his world. And he was very much in charge in his world. "It's a beautiful day. You should try to unwind a little. Go to the pool, or maybe try the whirlpool tub in your bathroom—"

"Cristiano," she said, cutting him short. "This isn't my home. I don't belong here."

"Why not?"

"Look around." She gestured, the sweep of her hand indicating the Palladian windows, mosaic flooring and soaring marble columns. "This is palatial, and if this is where Gabby will live, then good. But I can't live here. I…I'd feel lost. It's far too grand. I'm not a grand person. I'm a nanny. A simple country girl. You saw where I was raised."

"It might take some getting used to, but I think you'd be comfortable here. And safe."

"But what will I *do?* I've always worked, and with Gabby in school five days a week, I'll be at such loose ends. I'm not needed here—"

"Gabby needs you."

His words drew tears to her eyes. He'd said earlier in the week that it was she who needed Gabby, and he was right. And he'd also said that Gabby should be raised by her family, her real family, and he was right about that, too. Sam was grateful as a child for Mrs. Bishop's kindness, but what she really wanted, needed was her own family. Her own people. At least Gabby finally had her own. "She has you now, Cristiano. You are her family. Brother or father—it doesn't matter. You are what she needs."

"So you'd deny her a whole family?" he asked softly, and yet there was a thread of anger in his voice and she heard it. "You'll make her choose—a mother or a father? She can't have both?"

His anger stung her, and she hesitated, choosing her words more carefully. "She can have us both. We don't have to live in the same house."

"Then it's not a real family. It's her bouncing back and forth from one place to another, always packing a bag, and unpacking a bag. Is that what you want for her?"

It was close to the life Sam had known, at least the instability. "No." Sam bit her lip, felt her throat thicken. "I don't want her to have to juggle homes—lives. If I were her, I'd hate it."

"That was my life growing up. There was always something forgotten, something missing. The coat left at one apartment. The school papers lost at another. I hated it." Cristiano hadn't moved but she felt him so intensely, felt his energy and his focus. "My mother and father divorced when I was young. My mother lived in Cannes and my father in Monte Carlo and I was always traveling between." He took a breath. "Can't we do better for Gabriela?"

"But we're not married."

"Then maybe we should be."

"Cristiano." She looked at him, knowing that something had changed in the past twenty-four hours. She didn't know what had changed in him, but she saw it, felt it, from the moment they arrived at the airport to boarding his private jet in Manchester this morning.

Cristiano exuded power. Control. Outwardly he didn't look any different—same direct gaze, straight nose, sensual mouth—but he carried himself as though he were in charge.

And at the airport in Manchester, he took charge, meeting privately with his pilots, speaking to someone in air traffic control, inspecting the jet with his pilots before boarding.

As Sam observed Cristiano during the preflight process, it struck her that he didn't trust others. And he wasn't about to leave important details to others, either.

"I've done the marriage of convenience before, and it doesn't work." Sam said steadily. "In fact, I think it actually made Gabby's life worse."

"Impossible. If you weren't there, God knows where she'd be now. You've been her guardian angel from the beginning. If you hadn't been there during the kidnapping attempt, something tragic could have happened. If you weren't there to protect her from Johann, she'd be lost." He hesitated. "Would you prefer me to get down on one knee?"

Get down on one knee? My God, was he seriously proposing marriage? Sam's stomach somersaulted in a wild free form flip. "You're not asking me—"

"Marry me."

"You are." Her voice cracked.

"I will make sure you lack for nothing. I promise to take care of you the way you've taken care of Gabby, generously, patiently—"

The room had begun to spin. "I think I need to sit down."

He steered her to the right, to a comfortable sitting room overlooking the gardens. The room had been decorated in aqua tones, the furniture, silk drapes, and even the handwoven rug all pale blue and pale green, accented with touches of white like the seashells clustered on the mantel and the white long stemmed tulips spilling from vases on round tables.

Numbly, Sam sank onto one of the down-filled sofas. "I can't do this, Cristiano. I love Gabby, God knows I do, but I can't marry again, can't put myself through that again."

He reached inside his coat and withdrew an envelope. "What was the worst part of marriage?"

She stared, fascinated as he withdrew a sheet of folded paper. "Being trapped. Lacking financial independence."

Nodding, he unfolded the sheet of paper and held it out to her. "What if I'm willing to work with you on that?"

Puzzled, Sam took the paper. "How?" And then she looked down. Her eyes widened as she read. Her hand began to shake as she continued to the end of the document. "This is a…this is…"

"A prenuptial agreement. Just by marrying me you inherit a million pounds. If the marriage lasts a year, it's ten million—"

"No!" She dropped the paper on the couch, repulsed. "That's disgusting, *no*."

"Ten years and it's twenty million. If we had a child at any point, it's fifteen million—regardless of how long the marriage lasts—and the villa would of course be yours."

"Stop." Sam lurched to her feet, walked far from the couch, circling behind it. "Never mention it again." Her voice vibrated with fury. "I would never marry for money, never. I won't be bought."

"But you'd marry Johann and be poor?"

"It was to protect Gabby!"

"Protect her now and be secure."

"It's different—"

"What's different? The fact that I could actually provide for you? That I could afford to give you a good home and life? That I like you? That I'd enjoy your company? That I actually want you? Desire you? Need you in my bed?"

CHAPTER TEN

"STOP." She covered her ears, closed her eyes because he'd found the right arguments now, had found the very weapons to use against her.

She did love Gabriela and she'd discovered in Chester she enjoyed Cristiano's company. She'd probably enjoy life with Cristiano and Gabby very much.

Too much, especially considering Cristiano's wealth.

He had too much. He was too rich. Too famous. Too successful. Too powerful.

Sam wanted a simple life, needed a simple life, not this jetsetter's life in the south of France.

Sam lowered her hands, glanced at the prenuptial agreement still lying on the silver-blue linen couch. And standing where she was, with the sunlight slanting through the tall windows the couch was the same shade as the English sky in early April when it's no longer winter but not spring proper and the mornings are still crisp and cold but warm through the day.

That blue, that wispy sky-blue, was what her bridesmaids wore when she married Charles, too. She'd always loved blue. It was nature's favorite color.

"Charles was a priest," she said, her gaze fixed on the prenup. "He'd just finished his training when we married. He never thought of himself. He always put others first."

"Is that why you can't put yourself first? You don't think you deserve happiness?"

"That's not so—"

"You married Johann van Bergen."

"For Gabby, yes—"

"But think about it, Sam. You put everyone else's needs before your own. When do you finally get to be happy? When will it be your turn?"

She swallowed around the horrendous lump filling her throat. She hated his assessment, but there was also accuracy in his assessment. "You might not believe it, but I am happy. Happier, at least. This last week I've felt so much happier, and freer—"

"This last week?" He coughed, a hoarse grating sound. "Let's recap, shall we? This last week your husband deserted you, left you in financial ruins, forcing you to flee to England where you were trapped in a snowstorm, only to discover Gabby's not Johann's child and you're not even Johann's wife." His black brows pulled. He looked outraged. "This is your idea of better? *Santo Cielo*. Your life was worse than I thought."

It felt like he was trapping her with words and she shook her head frustrated.

"What has made you feel better? What has made you happier?"

"I don't know."

"Something must have changed. Something must have improved."

She started to shake her head and then she stopped, looked at Cristiano who was glaring at her in the worst scowl yet, and she knew.

It's you, she thought. *You've made it better.*

"What made it better?" he repeated, his gaze resting on her, his expression increasingly brooding.

"It's not important."

"It is to me."

"Why?"

"Why not?" he flared. "You've taken care of my sister. Maybe I want to take care of you."

"Well, you can't. I'm very good at taking care of myself—"

"I disagree. While you were assuming responsibility for a child that wasn't even yours, you were taken to the cleaners, financially and emotionally." His mouth compressed. "If you left here today. What would you do? Get another job? Find another nanny position?"

Sam blanched, swallowed, forced herself to nod. Because it's exactly what she'd do. It's what she'd have to do. She didn't have a choice. "Yes."

"And that's okay with you?"

"Maybe things would be tight financially, and maybe I'd be leaving my heart behind with Gabby, but I'd do what I have to do. I always have."

"Walk away from happiness?"

"No. Walk away from unhappiness. Because I am happier today than I was a week ago. It's a relief to have Johann gone. The villa we lived in was a rattrap. The pipes constantly leaked and there was mildew in the walls and there was never any money to fix things."

She balled her hands into fists, growing more livid by the second remembering. "Johann didn't want me. He married me to get Gabby, but marrying me meant he could also stop paying me. I'm thrilled we're not legally married. It was a horrible deal. I love Gabby but she has a real family now. I missed having an income, missed being financially independent, and now that I'm free, I'm not about to get into that situation again."

Cristiano clapped. "Bravo. Well done. I've been waiting for you to do that."

She glared at him. "Do what?"

"Stand up for yourself." The corners of his mouth tilted, creases fanned from his eyes. "And, Sam, you're right. Your home wasn't with Johann. Your home was with Gabby. Your home is still with Gabby. That hasn't changed. It will never change. She needs a mother, Sam, and you are that mother. You must know that in your heart."

He'd said all the right words, he'd said exactly what she felt. Sam loved Gabby as if she were her very own child.

"The prenuptial is intended to protect you, Sam. That's all. I don't want to buy you, or own you—"

"Then tear it up."

"Sam."

"Tear it up," she insisted.

He took the paper, shredded it and Sam exhaled. "I will marry you," she said quietly, "on one condition."

"What's that?"

She took a slow deep breath for courage. "That it be a real marriage. Not another marriage of convenience. I can't be a wife in name only anymore. I want to be a real wife. I want to be a real mom. I want to feel like I matter and I'm not just a contract or a piece of paper." And despite all her best efforts, her voice quavered. "The best part of marrying Charles was knowing I'd have a home, a place where I belonged. But then he died, it was all snatched away, it never happened."

Cristiano's hard jaw gentled. "I don't know your history with Charles, but I do know this. You belong here, Sam. We need you here—Gabby and me."

And that's when Sam gave up fighting, because she needed them even more.

They went back to Monte Carlo after dinner so Gabby could return to school. Cristiano notified Ludwin's School for Girls that Gabriela wouldn't be enrolling after all. Cristiano attended to business, leaving Sam to manage the wedding details. She could have any kind of wedding she wanted, he said, his only request was that it be soon.

Sam wanted a very small wedding and they settled on a private ceremony at the villa. There'd be no guests, just the three of them and the officiate, of course.

Planning the wedding was easy after that. Sam and Gabriela went shopping together in Monte Carlo, and Sam let Gabby select the dresses they'd wear for the afternoon ceremony. Gabriela was delighted to pick out a wedding dress for Sam and had Sam try on virtually everything in the store before finding a favorite.

Other details were attended to, like purchasing shoes to match their dresses—something Gabby felt was very important, and pretty hair accessories, again another Gabriela request.

But time had passed and it was Saturday afternoon, now just two hours before the ceremony. Cristiano had offered to send a hairdresser to the house but Sam thought that expense, on top of all the others, too frivolous. Instead she and Gabby holed up in Sam's bedroom suite at the villa where they sat in matching robes sharing afternoon tea before they changed into their special dresses.

"Are you scared, Sam?" Gabby asked, holding her cup delicately in one hand.

"I'm a little nervous," Sam admitted. "Marriage is very serious."

"Cristiano said you weren't really married to Papa Johann. That someone made a mistake and you were really just friends."

Sam was rather impressed with the explanation Cristiano had given Gabby. It wasn't the exact truth but it was one a child, particularly a sensitive child like Gabriela, could understand. "That's right. Johann and I are friends. We were never married like your friends' parents."

Gabby sipped from her cup. "Is that why you never shared the same bedroom?"

Sam flushed, embarrassed but not surprised that Gabby had picked up on that. "Yes."

"Will you and Cristiano share a bedroom?"

Sam's flush deepened. Her face felt hot from her neck to her scalp. "Probably," she hedged, stopped sipping. She hadn't thought about it. Deliberately hadn't thought about it.

"Will you and Cristiano have a baby?"

"Gabby." Sam rebuked softly. "Can Cristiano and I just get married first?"

"Okay." Gabby swung her legs, back and forth, while she looked past Sam to her pretty dress lying on the foot of the bed. "I knew he was going to come for us, didn't you?"

Sam felt the oddest sensation—half joy, half pain. "What do you mean?"

Gabby leaned forward to gently set her cup back in the saucer, taking great pains not to spill. "I always knew Cristiano would come. Didn't you?"

"No." Sam hesitated, nonplussed. "How did you know?"

"My angel."

Goose bumps covered Sam's arms. "You have an angel?"

"*Yes.* And so do you. Our angels are friends and do everything together and they knew since my mommy died, you'd be a good new mommy for me."

"Oh, Gabby—"

"I have a really good angel, too. Do you know who it is?"

Sam had never heard anything like this in her life. "Who?"

"My real dad. Enzo."

Blinking, Sam found herself wishing Cristiano were here.

"He died right before I was born so it makes sense," Gabby continued, sliding forward on her chair to reach for one of the miniature cakes frosted in pink and white icing. "Who do you think your angel is?"

"I haven't a clue."

"I think I know."

Sam was beginning to think this child was either brilliant or crazy. "Who?"

"Your Charles." Gabby looked up at her, and her expression shifted between fear and defiance. "And you can't cry anymore. He doesn't want you to cry. You're supposed to be happy now."

This was the oddest conversation to be having before a wedding, Sam thought. This was a conversation better suited to strong drink than strong black tea. "I had no idea you talked to angels this much."

"I talk to them a little bit. They talk to me more."

"And what do they say?" she asked carefully.

"That everything is going to be okay."

Surprised by the sudden welling of emotion, Sam bit her lip and realized that Gabriela had suffered far more than she let on, that the little girl had so many hopes and dreams and needs of her own.

Slipping off the chair, Gabby stripped off her robe. "Can we get dressed now?"

"Definitely," Sam answered, rising to help Gabby into her white organza dress.

While Gabby sat on the carpet to put her stockings and shoes on, Sam stepped into her own gown. It wasn't a dress Sam would have ever chosen for herself, the silk fabric the color of soft powdery sand, and the bronze bow a bit too much, but surprisingly when Sam tried the gown on in the bridal store, Sam loved it.

The gown was sleeveless, and the lace-crusted bodice clung to her breasts, shaped her waist and the full skirt fell in a romantic swirl of the palest, softest gold. Even the bronze silk bow, childish on the hanger, looked fresh and pretty when tied off-center.

Sam was so tempted to twirl in front of her bedroom mirror just to watch the fabric shimmer in the afternoon sun. The gown was beautifully cut but she loved the color best, loved the way the iridescent silk reminded her of water rushing over sand.

It was the perfect dress for Cap Ferrat, the perfect dress for being married privately in the villa's garden overlooking the sea.

Dressed, Sam combed Gabriela's curls, pinning some up, leaving others down until Gabriela looked like the princess she'd always wanted to be. And Sam, looking at her reflection in the mirror, thought simple was best and drew her long hair into a loose knot at her nape, before softening the style by pulling a few tendrils out. A little makeup, just a touch, and then pale gold shoes and gold and pearl chandelier earrings on her ears and she was ready.

Then just as Sam turned away from the mirror, a *whoosh* of air danced across the room. Both Sam and Gabby turned toward the balcony's open doors. A breeze was blowing the curtains at the windows and the white silky sheers fluttered.

"There they go," Gabby said, turning to Sam. "Our angels rushing through the sky."

And as the sheers fluttered again, Sam could almost picture Gabby's angels hurrying through the night.

Cristiano met them in the garden on the point. Wearing a classic black dinner jacket and slacks with an elegant white dress shirt, he looked gorgeous, and relaxed. But it was more than relaxed, Sam thought, taking Gabby's hand as they approached Cristiano and the officiate. He looked…happy.

There was no music, no processional, no ceremony to hide behind, and for that, Sam was grateful. She hadn't wanted anything that would detract from what they were doing. Or why they were doing it. Today was all about Gabby. They were starting a new life as a family, and they were putting Gabby first because it was a good and right thing to do.

Despite that knowledge, Sam felt a flurry of nerves as the vows were recited. She couldn't believe she was going to do this. She couldn't believe she was going to get married again. It was ludicrous. And thrilling.

She was stunned and overwhelmed. Hopeful and terrified. Nervous, emotional, tearful.

My God, she felt like a real bride.

And then the brief ceremony was over and a heavy ring weighted her finger and it was done.

They were married. Man and wife. Cristiano moved closer. He tipped her chin up to kiss her and Sam heard cheers and whistling but he then hesitated, his mouth so close to hers she could feel his warmth and smell his spicy clean fragrance.

Then she saw his lips curve and that brief, faint smile said everything and heat coursed through her. That smile of his was always her undoing, making her face burn and her lower lip throb and her body feel heavy and empty in a way it never had before. Then his head dropped and his lips covered hers and she felt a flare of bright white heat, her lips tingling.

The kiss was magical—sharp, hot, intense—and she was no longer at the villa but transported somewhere else, someplace that felt like heaven on earth. His arms circled her, brought her close, brought her against his hard frame and she felt him in a way she'd never felt him before.

He was so big, strong, and the shape of his body was new to her but welcome.

Sighing, she pressed closer and as his hand lingered low on her back shivers raced up and down her spine and she didn't want the kiss to ever end.

She'd never thought a man could make a woman feel so tender and so eager and so beautiful and so alive.

And then Cristiano was lifting his head and a trumpet sounded, followed by a violin and then an accordion. Tears filled Sam's eyes as she realized it was the villa staff members playing for them, the staff who'd brought instruments from home to give them music. The music was bright and joyful, celebratory and bittersweet and it was so unexpected, and so touching, that Sam couldn't hold the tears back.

"Signora Bartolo," Cristiano murmured, running his thumb beneath her eyes to dry her tears, "my staff and I welcome you home."

And with his arm still around her, he turned her to face his staff who'd gathered at the edge of the garden, many wearing their very best clothes, their faces wreathed with pleasure and tears continued to fill Sam's eyes.

"*Grazie,*" she said to Cristiano. "*Merci,*" she said to the French-speaking staff. And it was as beautiful a wedding day as she could have ever imagined.

But the celebration didn't end there. The villa's chef outdid himself preparing their wedding dinner. Considering there were only three of them, and one was a sleepy little girl, it was a gorgeous meal started off with hors d'ouvres of caviar and sour cream on blini, followed by mignon of beef tenderloin with garlic roasted eggplant and tomato basil brochette, and then finished with mixed greens with lobster, grilled artichoke hearts and carrots.

"This it too much food," Sam protested as the courses kept coming and Gabriella wandered away to locate Marcelle and find something more interesting to do than eat.

"As you can tell, Chef Sacchi is delighted you've decided to join our family."

They were sitting in the dining room and normally it was a huge formal space but villa staff had hung white and aqua chiffon panels from the ceiling creating a romantic tent. White lights were wrapped around bare tree branches and candles and white orchids glowed in the table center.

Cristiano took her hand, lifted it to his lips. "I'm delighted you've joined our family, although it's a very small family."

Sam's heart lurched at the brush of his lips across her skin. "Small families are good. Not quite so intimidating."

"Your family was small, too."

"Very."

"But at least we know family's important," Cristiano added, turning her hand over to kiss the inside of her wrist.

His kiss on her wrist was like fire licking her veins. She shivered, breathless, heart thumping, tension growing. She was scared. Scared of all she didn't know. Scared of all she'd never had. Scared of all she'd never done right.

And as his lips traveled across her inner wrist again, the fire raced from her wrist to her belly and legs, making her ache in places she hadn't thought she could ache. Somehow he made her feel so empty, empty and restless and she didn't know how to quiet the need.

She felt his gaze and sucked in a breath as she looked up into his face. In his eyes she saw hunger and interest.

He wanted her.

Sam shuddered again, goose bumps covered her skin. Her mouth dried, her heart slowed and it took an effort to clear her head, gather her thoughts, put a tight leash on her emotions.

"After we cut the cake, we'll be leaving the villa," Cristiano said, releasing her hand to refill her wineglass. "I've had our staff pack you an overnight bag so there's nothing you have to do."

"We're leaving the villa?"

"We can't very well honeymoon here."

"A honeymoon," she echoed faintly.

His gaze narrowed slightly, his expression revealing amusement. "It is our wedding night."

Oh, yes, back to all the things she didn't know. Sam's pulse quickened, fueled by nerves and fear and adrenaline. "What about Gabby?"

"Marcelle will be staying with her and all the villa staff dote on her. We won't be gone long. Just a night or two."

A night or two. Alone, all alone, with Cristiano. It wasn't a death sentence but it was terrifying.

Sam's head swam and it had nothing to do with the Pinot Noir they were drinking.

But before Sam could dissolve into puddles of panic, Chef Sacchi appeared from the kitchen rolling out a trolley with the most gorgeous three-tiered wedding cake Sam had ever seen.

The white-haired chef handed the decorated knife to Sam. "Madame," he said. "White chocolate cake filled with chocolate mousse, covered in white chocolate frosting and handcrafted gum paste seashells and roses."

Gabby came running back in followed by Marcelle who'd brought a camera.

And it struck Sam as Cristiano's hand covered hers and they cut the wedding cake together, that this was a real wedding, as real as her wedding to Charles all those years ago. Gabby begged for the edible shells and roses and Cristiano fed her a bite of cake, and as he put the piece between her lips, he let his fingertip linger on her bottom lip.

His touch made her tremble. She could barely get herself to chew and swallow.

"I think," he drawled, leaning close, "it's time we left and had a little time for ourselves."

Their honeymoon destination wasn't far. Cristiano had booked them one of the luxurious suites at the Hermitage in Monaco, where the famous five-star hotel dominated Square Beaumarchais and overlooked the port and the famous Winter Garden.

Sam had spent so much time with Cristiano away from crowds that she'd forgotten how the public responded to him. But the moment they stepped from his one-of-a-kind Italia Motors sports car in front of the Hermitage, to the moment they reached the door of their suite, people stopped, murmured, nodded, smiled, stared. Some even followed. One or two were bold enough to ask for autographs.

He was a huge celebrity. People knew him, and people were equally fascinated by him, and it jolted her more than a little. She'd remarried, and not just any man, but someone the public adored.

Inside their three-room suite, Cristiano locked the door and shrugged off his coat. In the living room the lights were already soft, music played from the suite's stereo system, and champagne chilled on ice.

Cristiano headed into the kitchen where vases of roses awaited them and a card from the hotel management welcoming Mr. and Mrs. Cristiano Bartolo to the hotel.

"Hungry?" Cristiano asked teasingly, swinging the refrigerator door open in the suite and revealing the platters of delicacies awaiting them—cheeses, patés, exotic fruits, chocolate-dipped strawberries.

Sam groaned, covered her eyes. "I can't even look at that. I think I'd die if I had to eat anything else."

He laughed appreciatively, drew two cold Perrier bottles out before letting the refrigerator door swing shut. "Should we check out the rest?" he asked, nodding toward the remaining rooms.

The bedroom was as big, if not bigger than the living room with two enormous walk-in closets, which prompted Sam to ask who actually had that many clothes, or wanted to travel with that many clothes, and then a blue marble bath with a huge whirlpool tub and a shower big enough for two.

"What do you want to do now?" he asked, sitting down on the edge of the huge bed and handing her one of the waters.

Nervously Sam twisted the cap from the green bottle. "Watch TV?"

"We could do that." He leaned across the bed, lifted the remote from the night table. "Come here. Help me find something to watch."

Cristiano heard her exhale softly, saw the tip of her tongue appear, saw her swallow. She was so nervous and she hesitated, one second, two seconds and then she moved toward him, her bridal gown swishing, the sleeveless lace top and full silk skirt reminding him of the dresses American girls wore to their high school dances. She looked just as young, too, and very unsure of herself.

Sam sat next to him on the bed, hands folding demurely in her lap. He leaned toward her, watched her lashes flutter close, her full mouth soften.

He brushed her mouth with his then lifted his head to measure her response. Her lashes lifted slightly. She looked up at him and her blue eyes were dark, mysterious, filled with unspoken wants and needs.

He kissed her again, slowly, so slowly that he felt her lips tremble against his. The heat between them flickered and flamed, exploding to life. The intensity startled her. He felt her resist, draw back. She would have pulled away, broken off the kiss, but he slid a hand into her long silky curls, crushing them with his hand, keeping her mouth pressed to his.

Her heart was beating harder now. He could feel the pulse in her throat, the throb in her veins. She was excited and yet afraid, but he understood that. Passion needed both. Passion required intensity, risk and the unknown.

He deepened the kiss, increasing pressure against her mouth and her lips quivered then opened beneath his. Her lips were soft, and her breath was warm and she tasted like Tuscany in the summer—warm, ripe, sweet.

He stroked the inside of her mouth with his tongue, teased her silken inner lip, flicked the tip of his tongue across the crease of her lips, sucked her tongue into his mouth, applying pressure until she whimpered, her hands kneading his chest, fingers curling into his skin.

Her soft muffled whimper nearly shattered his self-control. Reaching over, he scooped her up, into his arms and drew her firmly down onto his lap to feel her warmth on his legs, the curve of her bottom on his heavy erection.

"*Bella,* Samantha," he whispered against her mouth, one hand against her jaw, fingers spread taut across the curve of bone and the softness of her cheek.

Sam shuddered at the pleasure of the kiss. No one had ever touched her the way he did, no one had ever made her feel beautiful and alive like this.

Reaching up, she clasped the back of his neck, her fingers twining in his thick hair that touched his collar. Charles's kisses had always been so chaste, so safe and controlled, but this kiss leveled her, this kiss proved how little she knew of life, and love, and men.

He was kissing her mouth again, teaching her how to play, how to tease, how to make her want him.

But the kissing wasn't enough. Sam wanted more and she arched against him, and as she arched, she felt his hand cover her breast, first cupping the fullness then palming the nipple. The longer he touched her breast, the more fire she felt race through her veins. He was making her feel wild inside, making her feel hot and explosive from her breasts all the way to between her legs.

He continued to touch her, stroking beneath her breast, down her rib cage, low to her hip, then up again. And as he stroked slowly back up, he rediscovered her breast, lingered over her taut nipple.

She felt sensitive, so sensitive and Sam writhed at the merciless attention. Her lower abdomen felt so tight it was almost uncomfortable and she shifted again on his lap, moving her hips in a restless, unconscious rhythm.

"Cristiano," she groaned against his mouth, not sure if it was a plea or a protest. He was making her feel at so many levels, and she could think of nothing but feeling more.

With one hand he began to unfasten the first of the dozen tiny buttons on the back of her dress while he caressed her hipbone and thigh with the other. It was maddening, the touches. While her dress began to slowly open, Cristiano teased and tormented her inner thighs. She clenched and unclenched her legs, felt wanton for wanting his hand between her thighs, then frightened of giving herself up to him.

Patiently he worked his way down the back of her gown, lower and lower. Sam could feel the cool air on her shoulders and back. She hadn't worn a bra as a bustier had been stitched into the bodice to provide shape and support and now that he'd opened the gown at the back he could peel the bodice away from her breasts.

He drew her to her feet, stood her between his knees and slowly tugged the gown off her breasts, over her waist and down her hips.

She was wearing a very simple cream lace garter and panty and nothing else. Sam blushed, looked away, incredibly self-conscious.

Cristiano caught her chin in his hand and turned her face to his, forcing her to look at him. "You are the most beautiful woman I've ever known."

"No—"

"Yes." He drew her toward him, folding her into his arms so that her breasts were crushed against his shirt. "Yes, Signora Bartolo. Trust me on this one. I know."

CHAPTER ELEVEN

FROM there, things moved quickly, although Cristiano had fully intended to take it slow. And he had been taking it slow, even after he'd peeled her gown off, exposing Sam's gorgeous full breasts and her small waist and the rounded hips that made her all woman.

Lying back, he drew her down next to him, sliding his hands from her breasts down her ribs, over her hips and up again. She arched as he swept the warm soft length of her, arched and whimpered as his hands explored the small of her back and then the ripe curve of her pert derriere.

As she pressed herself against him, he groaned deep in his throat. *Santo Cielo,* did this woman have any idea what she was doing to him?

He wasn't a saint, not like her. He did what he wanted, took what he needed, gave what he could. No more, no less. He didn't live for others, had given up years ago trying to please others, and yet with Sam it was different. Luscious English Samantha made him want to turn the world upside down to please her.

Her skin glowed hot beneath his hands and he measured each of her ribs then down over her flat taut belly. Wife, he thought, fingers brushing the apex of her thighs. My wife. My woman.

She shifted as his fingers explored her, shyly opening her knees for him and the blood roared in Cristiano's ears, drumming through his body. He was so hard he hurt, so turned on he felt

dangerous. There was no more slow and gentle. He wante_ ner. Needed her. Was determined to possess her, thoroughly, completely so there could be no doubt she was now his.

Cristiano didn't remember shedding his clothes but they were gone and he was rolling her beneath him, his hand parting her knees, teasing the satin skin of her thighs and then the even softer satin skin between her thighs. She was wet, warm and so damn willing.

And it wasn't until he'd entered her, thrusting into her very tight body and he heard her gasp, that he realized he'd hurt her and his desire to possess her faded in the face of her pain.

"Sam," he whispered, holding still, afraid to move for fear of inflicting more hurt. "*Bella,* what did I do?"

Her small hand stroked his back. "Nothing."

But he felt the tension in her, her slender thighs taut on either side of his hips.

"I'm sorry," he whispered, smoothing her long blond hair back from her face as he kissed her mouth and then her jaw and the soft skin beneath her ear. "I'm sorry. I thought you were ready."

Her blue gaze met his and there was no anger there, no blame, either. "I was ready."

"But I did hurt you."

"It always hurts the first time, doesn't it?"

For a moment he didn't understand and then still buried in her body, awareness dawned. He pushed up on his elbows to take the weight of his body off her. "You're—"

"Yes, but it's okay." She reached for him, clasped his face in her hands and brought his head down to hers. "I couldn't be one forever," she murmured against his mouth.

"I should have known," he protested. "You should have told me."

"Told you what? That I'm a virgin?"

"But you've been married."

"Yes, twice. Well, three times in a way." She tried to make a joke of it so they could move on. "Says a lot for my sex appeal, doesn't it?" But before he could answer, she kissed him again, kissed suggestively, tracing his lip with her tongue until she felt the spark between them again, the sharp electric heat that was both hot and maddening.

His body throbbing in hers, he began to move, slowly, giving her time to adjust to him and little by little she could take him even deeper and she did. He seemed to want as much of her as he could, as much of her as she'd give.

Sighing, she wrapped her legs around him, felt him bury deeper, felt the last lingering discomfort give way to pleasure and interest.

As he stroked her with his body, Sam pressed her face to his chest, she wrapped her legs around his hips and breathed him in. She loved the feel of his skin on hers, the warmth, the pressure, the sensation. It was all wonderful, she thought, his scent, the hard planes of his muscles, his strength.

She loved the way he drove his body into hers, and as he moved in her, with her, she discovered how the pleasure just grew. She'd never been this close to anyone, couldn't imagine doing this with anyone else but with Cristiano it felt right.

Being in his arms, with his body joined with hers, she felt safe, cherished. *Loved.*

And the feeling of love intensified, tightening, strengthening until it exploded, shaping and reshaping into something bigger and brighter than she'd ever felt.

It was an orgasm, she knew that much, but it wasn't what she'd thought it would feel like. She'd always thought an orgasm would feel well, physical. Sexual. But this pleasure, this release, was gorgeous and emotional, sensual and spiritual. She'd never felt so close to anyone as she did to Cristiano just then, and as she shuddered in his arms, her body rippling around his, she was part earth, part universe, a comet streaking across the sky before dropping like stardust into the sea.

She was still sensitive, still shuddering at the intense pleasure when Cristiano groaned and came deep inside of her.

Cristiano held her close against him and he was so quiet she thought he must have fallen asleep but when she stirred to go to the bathroom, Cristiano took her hand in his and brought it to his mouth, kissing the back of her hand. "I'm sorry I hurt you."

She turned on the bed, looked down at him, moonlight playing across the bed. "You didn't hurt me. You made me feel wonderful."

"I'd never hurt you, Sam. You're to be cherished."

She leaned over and kissed him. "I'm glad you were my first lover. I hope you're my last. I can't imagine being with anyone else now."

He made a rough sound, primitive and raw, and dragged her closer to his side. "Good," he grunted. "I shouldn't like to think of my wife fantasizing about other men."

Early that morning they made love again, Cristiano taking time to teach her, encourage her, compliment her. "There are no rules between a man and woman in bed. If you trust one another, respect one another, everything's good, everything's right. It's a matter of being comfortable and communicating."

"You know a lot about sex," she said, trying not to be jealous of the history he had before her but not quite succeeding.

He smiled and drew her on top of him, introducing her to yet another position. "What can I say? I'm Italian. We enjoy women. But now you're my wife."

Later they ordered breakfast in bed and napped after their late breakfast and then Cristiano carried her into the shower where he introduced her to a few more new things.

Later, taking him in her hand, she relished soaping him up and down, using the excuse of showering to get to know his body better.

But when her soapy hand brushed one of his thighs he stiffened, caught her hand, moved it away.

"Did I hurt you?" she asked.

"No." He adjusted the shower nozzle so the water didn't splash her face or in her eyes.

"Do they ever hurt? The burns?"

"Yes." It was his turn to lather his hands and begin applying the suds to her body.

"Is that why you don't want me to touch you there?"

"No." Dropping his head, he brushed his mouth across her lips. "I just don't think you need to touch something like that."

Sam grabbed the soap away from him, pushed him back from her so she could see him clearly. "We're talking about you. *Your* legs."

"Exactly."

"I like your legs."

"Sam, *bella*—"

"No. No, *bella*, no Sam. Listen to me—"

"I am and you sound like my nanny now."

She ignored his complaint, moving closer to him so she could kiss his shoulder. "I like you," she murmured against the muscular plane of his chest, "and I like your legs, so I'm going to touch you where I want, and how I want, because that's what you do for me."

Then without waiting for permission, she slid her hands across the front of his thighs, feeling the thick scars and the uneven texture, the skin a complex map of seams, hollows and ridges, before circling to the back of his legs. The skin had been burnt there, too, but the scarring wasn't quite as thick and she felt the long thin surgical scar she'd seen that afternoon at the cottage.

Cristiano stood stiffly while she touched him, his head averted, silently suffering through her gentle exploration. But as her hands circled back around, hands clasping his shaft, he became very hard, very fast and after a minute of gritting his teeth, he turned her around, parted her legs, made sure she was wet and then with a slow, smooth thrust into her, introduced her to yet another of his favorite positions.

Finally worn-out, they both slept and when they woke, Cristiano let Sam have the bath to herself for a long hot soak in the tub. When she emerged, still wrapped in two fluffy towels, he surprised her with a large wrapped gift box.

"Something special for you to wear tonight," he said.

Sam tore open the wrapping paper, pulled off the top of the

box and pushed aside the lilac tissue to discover a puddle of blue-gray fabric, a beaded evening bag of the same color, and a pair of high heel sandals that laced around her ankles.

The dress was little more than a silk slip with delicate spaghetti straps and a softly shirred bodice that plunged deeply, nearly all the way to the high empire waist. Sam dropped her towel, stepped into the dress and after adjusting the slender straps, let Cristiano zip it at the back for her.

It was a perfect fit. The color made her skin glow creamy-gold and the short hem, hitting several inches above her knees, highlighted her slender legs.

Sam had pulled the towel off her still-damp hair and she started to pin it up but Cristiano pulled her hands away. "Leave it down. Let me see you. I love to look at you."

"My hair will be too curly if I don't style it."

"I love the curls. You—your hair—it's all perfect."

Coloring, she shook her head, feeling shy despite the intimacy between them. "I'm not perfect, Cristiano. Far from it."

"In my eyes you're perfect."

"Maybe it's because you don't know me very well yet."

He took her hand, drew her to him, shaped her hips to his so that she felt him, and felt his hunger and desire and pleasure. "I will always think you're perfect because I know you are perfect for me."

The compliment warmed her, but it was the caress of his hand beneath her dress where he cupped her breast, and then pinched her nipple that inflamed her.

Sam stood on tiptoe and kissed him, a deep, erotic kiss where she sucked the tip of his tongue the way he'd kissed her yesterday and sliding her hands down his chest, over his flat abdomen she stroked his erection through his trousers. She could feel him grow beneath her touch, feel him strain against the fabric and emboldened, she unzipped his pants, took him out, caressed him with her hands and then kneeling, put her mouth on him, trying something new of her own.

It was much later when they finally left their room to have an early evening drink in one of the hotel's elegant lounges.

Even though she was sitting with a famous, gorgeous man in a sophisticated bar, Sam had never felt more comfortable in her life.

Cristiano somehow knew how to put her at ease. It was just the way he talked to her, looked at her, smiled at her. Even from the beginning he'd made her feel special, different, and now after thirty-six hours alone in a hotel room with him, she felt even better.

She smiled shyly at him, the bar's great chandeliers splashing light here and there like a glittering ball gown. He was, she thought, smiling even bigger, perfect for her, too. Not because he was rich, or famous, or even heartbreakingly gorgeous, but because he treated her so well and he made her feel like the most beautiful woman in the world.

And no one, not even dear good Charles, had ever made her feel beautiful.

Kind, yes. Patient, yes. Gentle, yes. But sexy? Interesting? *Fun?*

Cristiano reached across the table, ran his thumb along the curve of her lips. "You're smiling."

"I know." And she could even feel her eyes smile. "I'm just so happy."

For a moment he said nothing and then he said in a surprisingly husky voice. "You should always be happy. You deserve to be happy."

With two hours still before their dinner reservations Cristiano slid his arm around Sam and they went for a leisurely walk through the Hermitage's Italian loggia, and then on to the Hotel de Paris where they were to have dinner later at the famous Le Louis XV.

Le Louis XV was the most prestigious restaurant in the city. Between Alain Ducasse's superb menu and the restaurant's opulent golden interior, it was impossible to dine at Louis XV and not be dazzled.

As they were escorted to their table at ten, Sam noted that the restaurant was packed, every table full, and there were dozens of chic people still hoping to get lucky and get a reservation for the night.

Dinner was lovely, Cristiano couldn't have been more attentive and after they'd finished their meal, they shared the restaurant's classic dessert, Crepes Suzette which had been created nearly a hundred years earlier for Edward VII, the then Prince of Wales, and his mistress.

On their way out, several people stopped Cristiano to congratulate him and or wish him well. By the time they escaped the restaurant and stepped outside, Sam marveled at Cristiano's patience with the interruptions. He was obviously used to being a public figure. It was new for her, and frankly uncomfortable, but she admired the way he handled himself—cordial, sincere, even if not particularly loquacious.

Back in their suite at the Hermitage, they made love slowly taking time to build the pleasure and tension, and after they reached orgasm, Cristiano drifted off to sleep, his arm wrapped protectively around Sam. And even though Sam was tired, and not surprisingly, sore, she couldn't sleep.

She was too warm on the inside. Too full of thoughts and memories. Memories of her life before Cristiano and it stunned her, how much he'd changed her life in less than four weeks.

She'd fallen for him so hard. And already she trusted him so much, depending on him for a dozen things she'd never depended on anyone for. At least not since her parents died.

She felt a niggle of alarm. Everything was too good, too happy, too lovely. This couldn't be real. Happiness like this never lasted. It was romance—passion— maybe just plain old lust, but it wasn't love. Couldn't be love. She didn't know Cristiano well enough, or long enough. Their attraction was chemistry and sex, very good sex, but wasn't that all it was?

No. This wasn't sex. She knew it wasn't just sex. She admired Cristiano, had only fallen for him after she'd seen how he interacted with Gabriela. She loved his strength and patience with his sister, loved his determination to take care of her and protect her.

And that was why she was afraid. Because all the good feelings, all her tenderness and love made her realize how starved she'd been for love.

Scarcity.

Lying close to Cristiano, Samantha admitted how empty she'd been, how hopeless she'd become. Looking back on the past eight years she could have been a feudal peasant during a time of plague or famine. She keenly felt the lack of all she'd been deprived of.

It wasn't that she wanted to feel sorry for herself. She was grateful for Charles. Charles had been wonderful, so kind, so caring—generous to a fault—for wasn't it his generosity that put him in danger?

After he died she tried to do what he would have wanted. She tried to follow his example, tried hard to be as good, and selfless, and kind as he had been. But she wasn't by nature so altruistic. Not that she wanted to be selfish, but she'd had so little of her own, so little time and attention, so little emotional support that on the inside she felt downright drained. Depleted.

Scarcity.

She'd become a woman who thought in terms of hunger, who trusted nothing, was famished—starved—for more. And she hadn't even known she'd been so starved until now when she'd had this heady taste of comfort and warmth and sensation.

And that was her terror—her need was huge. She couldn't bear to ever be that empty and hungry again. But she wasn't sated, not yet, not by a long shot. She was still starved, starved for more, starved for abundance and secretly it horrified her, just how great her need was.

If this time with Cristiano didn't last, if this closeness and warmth disappeared, what would she do then?

She couldn't let herself rely too heavily on him, couldn't let herself become too vulnerable. She had to know that comfort—closeness—never lasted.

Her parents had loved her and they'd died. Charles, who'd loved her, died. She didn't have to be a rocket scientist to see a pattern here. Anyone who might love her would leave or perish. Fighting panic, Sam scooted out from beneath his arm, slipped from the bed and realizing she couldn't find any of her real clothes, picked up one of the hotel towels still tossed over the chaise lounge in the bedroom corner and wrapped it around her.

Covered in the towel, Sam went to the living room, opened the balcony door and stepped outside. Breathe, she told herself, just breathe.

She took long slow, deep breaths until her heart stopped racing and the panic eased. She wasn't starving now, not this moment. She wasn't alone right now. Cristiano was just inside, in bed. *Don't anticipate the worst,* she reminded herself. *Focus on the moment.* ·

Leaning on the balcony railing she looked out and around. It was the middle of the night but the city was still alive. For a few minutes Sam watched the cars and taxis below until she turned toward the ocean. Far out the horizon was dark but close to the harbor, illuminated yachts bobbed.

"Can't sleep?" Cristiano's voice sounded behind her.

Warmth filled her, warmth and delight. Leaning on the balcony Sam flashed him a welcoming smile. "No. My head's spinning too much."

"Too much champagne?"

"Too much you."

"Impossible." He stepped outside to stand beside her. The night had grown cool and when she shivered he wrapped an arm around her and brought her close. "I'm good for you."

She looked up at him over her shoulder. "I was never going to get married again. This is all your fault, you know."

"Marriage doesn't have to be a losing proposition, Sam. Good things can happen in relationships."

"If marriage is so wonderful, Cristiano, why did you wait until now to get married?"

"Timing." He kissed the top of her head. "And fate."

"So you've never met anyone you even considered marrying?"

When he didn't answer immediately, she knew she had her

answer. But she didn't rush him and eventually he answered. "There was someone once, but the timing couldn't have been worse."

"So it ended?"

"Yes."

"And we're together because you got tired of waiting for the right woman to come along," she concluded.

"No. We're together because of fate." He scooped her into his arms and began walking back toward the bedroom. "And now we're together because it's late, and I'm tired, and we're going to bed."

In the big bed with the soft down pillows, Sam nestled close to Cristiano's warm chest. She'd only been with him two days and yet she already had her favorite place to be. And if she was scared, it was only because she couldn't bear the thought of ever being without him. The last time she'd been held like this, she'd been just a child, not much more than Gabby's age.

"Thank you, Cristiano, for everything," she whispered.

He kissed her temple, smoothed her hair. "Sleep, *bella*. There's a little girl anxious to see you in the morning, and trust me, she won't care if you haven't slept in days."

The next morning they returned to the villa in Cap Ferrat and yes, Gabby was thrilled to see them. She danced around their legs as they walked from the car to the house and finally Cristiano picked her up to keep from stepping on her. "You're as bad as a puppy," he teased.

Gabby responded with a big lick on the side of his face.

Cristiano groaned and Sam laughed quietly thinking she'd been right, about those thoughts she'd had on the plane. Nothing was the same. Not for Gabby, not for her, not for any of them. But they did adapt, slowly settling into a new routine where they spent the work week in Monte Carlo and Cristiano's penthouse apartment and then weekends and school holidays at the villa.

It was a relatively easy commute and Sam and Gabby loved the villa best. It was always such a treat to return to the villa after five days in the city.

It was nearly the end of January and with February approaching Sam knew she had to do something about Gabby's party but wasn't sure where to even begin.

"Call an event planner," Cristiano told her when she confessed to him one evening that she was nervous about throwing a big party. Married to Johann they'd never had money to do a proper party and yet Sam knew that some of the parties Gabby had attended were incredibly lavish.

"That'll cost a fortune," Sam told him, crawling into bed after checking on Gabby once more for the night.

"Money's not an issue," he answered, "and you did promise her a real party. It's her fifth birthday after all."

"I know, but spending huge amounts of money on five-year-olds doesn't really make a lot of sense."

"It's not about the money, Sam. It's about giving Gabriela something special to remember."

And Sam knew that, but one of the hardest transitions for her in married life was this concept of spending freely. She'd never had extra money. It was a necessity to be frugal and fifteen years later it was a very hard habit to break. "You honestly don't mind me putting on a big party for Gabby?"

"I'd be disappointed if you didn't. This has been a traumatic year for her. I'd like nothing better than for her to have an absolutely magical fifth birthday."

"So clowns, face painters, trained dogs…that's all okay?"

"Acrobats, jugglers, magicians. No problem."

"What about elephants?"

Cristiano grabbed Sam, rolled her beneath him and kissed her until she melted against him. "No elephants," he growled when he finally lifted his head. "And let's skip the tigers, too."

He dipped his head to kiss her once more and it didn't take long for the sweet, playful kiss to spark into hot, explosive desire.

CHAPTER TWELVE

SAM hired an event planner Chef Sacchi had worked with when he was the head pastry chef at the La Palme d'Or in Cannes and after the event planner visited the villa, saw the space for the party and heard the circus theme, he promised he could create something fantastic that would thrill children and adults alike.

"We shall do our own Festival du Cirque Monte-Carlo, yes?" The theatrical young man said. "A tent, a marquee, red carpet and of course the circus acts."

"My husband has only two stipulations," Sam said. "No elephants—they would be hard on the gardens, and no tigers. If one escaped he knows the neighbors would complain."

"Ah, yes, a wise husband." The young man nodded his head thinking. "We can pass on the exotic animals but I can maybe find you a small elephant, one not so big it'd crush the daffodils."

Sam fought the desire to smile. "I'm sorry. Cristiano was really quite clear. No elephants, but I think the children would love small ponies."

Two days after trucks began to line the villa driveway as scores of workers from the different party rental companies set to work constructing the circus tent, the center ring and the bleacher seating. Lights were strung inside the white tent and more lights were strung outside the tent. A great cobalt-blue sign with fancy gold lettering that had been hand-painted just for the occasion was hung outside the tent, Festival du Cirque Gabriela, and in the middle was a big gold number 5.

Weeks earlier the invitations had been hand delivered by a courier, the red and white striped envelopes with red and gold card stock inviting the children and their parents to Gabriela Bartolo's fifth birthday party. Sam had feared many children wouldn't drive from Monte Carlo to the villa in Cap Ferrat for the party, but there was only one regret and that was a last minute cancellation when a little girl came down sick.

The event planner didn't forget anything. He brought in food stalls to offer guests everything from cotton candy to croque monsieur and croque madame, hired a half dozen of the best clowns in Europe and even imported a small antique carousel the children could ride amid flashing, swirling lights.

The circus party was a gigantic hit. Gabby stood with Sam and Cristiano in front of the roaring white tent as guests arrived, greeting each of her friends from school with delight. As the children and their parents followed the red carpet into the tent, through the entrance's black and white striped poles, Gabby could hardly contain herself.

Once the guests had all arrived the circus began with a welcome from the circus' ringmaster, a short stout gentleman wearing a red coat, black pants and boots. He wore a top hat and carried a whip but promised the children he wouldn't use it if they were good, which elicited squeals from the children and then fresh squeals when a white-faced clown with a hat many sizes too small ran out into the ring chasing a small dog. The dog jumped into the ringmaster's startled arms and then jumped out and barking frantically dashed in and out of the stands before disappearing again.

And that was just the beginning.

There were acrobats, trapeze artists, white Austrian horses and Spanish dancers. Clowns chased each other into the stands, tumbled out of miniature cars, sprayed one another with water and tried to get pigs to dance and dogs to talk and by the time the ringmaster reappeared at the end to thank the children for coming, and to invite them into the center ring for cake, Gabby was speechless with awe.

After the cake was cut and eaten, the children and parents began to depart. Within a half hour nearly everyone was gone and the cleanup crew began breaking down the tent. "I loved my circus," Gabby said wistfully, as the canvas tent was peeled off the poles.

"It was a good party," Sam agreed.

Nodding, Gabby yawned and leaned against Sam's leg. Cristiano saw the yawn, too, and he stooped to pick up Gabby. He straightened and turned toward the house, but not before Sam had seen him wince. He was in pain again.

"I can take her," Sam offered and Cristiano shot her a hard glance.

"I have her," he said.

They set off for the villa, Gabby's head on Cristiano's shoulder, her eyes half-closed. Cristiano wasn't walking slower than usual but he was certainly favoring his right leg a little more but Sam said nothing to him about it knowing it would only irritate him. He never discussed the injury, never talked about pain, either, but she knew he felt it, lived with it, and there were times she wished she could do something for him—more for him—but Cristiano was proud. There were things, like his accident, he just wouldn't share.

Gabby fell asleep early that night worn-out from the big day, and Sam and Cristiano had dinner in their room, and watched the evening news from their bed.

As the news program moved from world news to local news, and economic and current events to sports and entertainment, the announcer mentioned a tragic loss in the sporting world: thirty-one-year-old Nils Hiukka, two-time Indy 500 winner died in Phoenix, Arizona, that morning after a tire failure during a practice run sent him into a concrete wall.

Cristiano reached for the remote control and abruptly turned the television off before tossing the control onto the nightstand.

Sam looked at Cristiano. "You knew him?"

"Yes."

She waited for him to say more, but he didn't. He simply stood, headed for the bathroom where he stripped off his clothes and stepped into the shower.

Sam was already in bed with the lights out when Cristiano returned. She heard him flip the covers back on his side, felt the mattress give beneath his weight, and then he was behind her, pulling her toward him.

"You're upset," she murmured.

"He was a former teammate."

Cristiano fell silent, and as the silence stretched, she felt the room grow cold, the bed empty. He was there, but not, and his arms might be around her, but he'd detached, disappeared from her.

"Cristiano," she whispered his name as she turned in his arms to face him. His eyes were open and he was staring at a place past her head. "When were you on the same team?"

"Ten years ago. Before I drove for Italia Motors."

He fell silent again and she bit her lip, hoping he'd soon talk, tell her more but he didn't. He remained strangely silent and reserved, so unlike the Cristiano she'd come to know.

After several minutes Sam reached up and touched his mouth with her fingertips. He was so beautiful, his nose was long, perfectly straight, his chin squared, and his mouth with that curve in his upper lip, the lower lip firm, sensual. She loved his face. She'd never get tired of looking at him. "What are you thinking?" she asked gently.

For a moment she didn't think he'd answer, and then he exhaled slowly. "About my father." Cristiano turned his head, looked at her. "He liked Nils, but he used to say that Nils's enthusiasm overruled his judgment."

"Nils was reckless?"

"His tactics bordered on reckless, yes."

"What kind of driver was your dad?"

"Brilliant." There was no hesitation on Cristiano's part. "I realize you don't know anything about racing, but my father was one of the greatest drivers of all time. Less than ten years ago he won thirteen Grand Prix in one year—Australia, Malaysia,

Bahrain, San Marino, Spain, United States, Monaco—you name it. He won it. Before he died, he won four World Championships—only Juan-Manuel Fangio of Argentina won more, and that was in 1950s."

He was right, she didn't know anything about racing but she was impressed. "Your father sounds remarkable."

"People always wanted to know his secret, and there wasn't a secret to his success. It was just him. His personality. Behind the wheel he was always cool, calm, unflappable. But he was incredibly strong. He won because he didn't tire—physically or mentally."

Sam slid up Cristiano's torso, pressed a light kiss to his chin and then his lip. "He taught you to drive?"

"Yes." His lashes flickered down, and then up again. The corner of his mouth lifted in a small, rueful smile. "It's funny. As a driver he was cool and calm, as a father he could be short-tempered. I think he resented anyone or anything that took him away from the track."

"He must have traveled a lot."

"He lived to race. He didn't care what he drove, either. He'd race anything—Corvettes, Ferraris, F1s, Champcars, oval racers, even long distance sports car races."

"Did you ever go with him, on those trips?"

"No. My parents divorced when I was young, and I was sent to boarding school. I hated it. All I wanted to do was race, too. My dream was to someday drive with Dad. To make his team. And then when I was twenty-six I won the French GP and Italia Motors—my father's team—signed me."

"You must have been thrilled."

He laughed faintly. "Over the moon. But of course I didn't get to race with him right away. I was the third team member, which meant I did a lot of sitting and waiting for my turn. I hated sitting, I'm a Bartolo after all, but a year later, here in Monaco for the Grand Prix, an injury to the second team driver opened up a spot for me. I took second that day, my father took first, and I never had to sit as an alternate again."

"So you helped each other win?"

"Teammates look out for each other. It's what you do."

Sam heard his voice deepen and she glanced up into his eyes. Cristiano's hazel-green eyes were shadowed with pain.

"I'm sorry Gabby will never know him," he said huskily. "She should have known him. He would have enjoyed her tremendously."

"You said he died just months before she was born."

"Four months before she was born. In October. At the Brazilian Grand Prix."

Sam heard the heartbreak in his voice and it reminded her of the grief she'd seen in his eyes back in Cheshire. And not just grief, but remorse.

Sam chewed on her thumb and looked at Cristiano, studying his thick dark hair, his incredible cheekbones, and the most beautiful mouth in the whole world. "Tell me," she said softly.

"Tell you what?"

"Tell me what hurts."

"You already know my legs hurt."

She pinched his chest, just above his nipple. "I'm not talking about your legs. I'm talking about the other things, the hurt inside you."

He lifted a hand, smoothed his palm over her hair, letting the curls coil around his fingers. "Sorry, *bella*. Men don't talk that way."

"Why not?"

"Because it's not—" his eyes briefly glinted, a flash of humor "—masculine."

She smiled wryly and then her smile faded and she leaned closer to his chest, letting her heart beat against his. "Your dad died at the race in Brazil."

"Yes."

"And it still makes you sad."

"Yes."

"It was an accident, wasn't it?"

"Yes."

Sam heard the catch in his deep voice and her eyes closed,

her hands open on his shoulders. She could feel his pain. She could feel it as strong as anything and she was almost afraid to touch him. To be so close to someone and know how much they hurt.

To know you couldn't save or heal, change or fix. All one could do was listen. And care.

Care. God, she cared. She cared so much she thought she'd die if anything happened to him. For the first time in eight years she felt like a real person again, she felt whole and happy and for the first time since Charles died, she knew she'd have a long, normal life. With Cristiano. With Gabby. Her family.

But she wanted to comfort Cristiano, comfort him the way he'd comforted her and yet she didn't know what to say, didn't understand the racing world, or why anyone would want to race in the first place. Cars terrified her. They were dangerous. Car accidents had taken three people she loved. Cristiano's own father had died in a race. Cristiano's friend had died practicing for a race.

"I'm glad you don't race anymore," she said, gently stroking his chest. "So glad that's behind you—"

"But it's not." He caught her hand, stilled it on his chest. "I still race. I never retired."

"But you haven't been driving…"

"We're off season but I still drive every day, Sam."

"I thought you've been going to your office."

"Yes, after I go to the track."

She struggled to free herself but he held on to her wrist. "You never told me."

"You never asked."

She tugged harder on her wrist. "How could I ask something I didn't know?" she cried.

"But you know who I am! You know what I do. This is how I pay the bills, Sam. I have sponsors, a team, endorsements—"

"You also have an international driving school."

"Which is something I enjoy and am proud of. But I'm a driver. I love to compete."

"Even though racing killed your father?"

Cristiano's brow furrowed. His jaw tensed. He released her and let her roll away. "I am a Bartolo, Sam. I will always be a Bartolo."

She sat up on the side of the bed, her heart racing, hot tears burning the back of her eyes. "And what does that mean?"

"It means I love to drive fast. Cars—engines—speed, it's in my blood. And Gabriela's blood, too. We're the same—"

"No."

"Yes, and you might not like it, but you're going to have to accept it. I'm *not* Charles. I've never wanted to serve others. All I ever wanted was to race. That's it."

"And be on your dad's team."

"And I am."

Furious tears stung her eyes. "Even though he's gone?"

"I can still carry on his name—"

"Not if you die in some accident!"

"I've already nearly died in some horrific accident. But I'm not going to quit. I will never quit."

"You won't have to quit. You'll die first!" And she left the bedroom then, grabbed clothes from the dresser on her way out, determined to go elsewhere, sleep elsewhere, determined to escape the fire and fear burning inside her heart.

Sam ended up sleeping in one of the guest rooms, although she didn't actually fall asleep until three. It was late when she woke up, and the villa was quiet.

Going downstairs Sam bumped into Marcelle in the kitchen. "Where is Gabby?" Sam asked, putting the kettle on for tea.

"With Mr. Bartolo."

"Are they in the garden?"

"No, Madame. They're at the *Automobile Monegasque*, but should be back in an hour for lunch."

Sam had a cold sick sinking feeling in her gut. "What is the *Automobile Monegasque?*"

"The track, Madame."

"Track?"

"Um, the facility where Monsieur practices." Marcelle held her hands up as if on an imaginary steering wheel. "Practices…drives."

"Yes, I understand." But Sam didn't. At least she didn't understand why Cristiano was there now, on a Sunday morning, with Gabby in tow. "I just didn't—" She broke off, swallowed her criticism. "Is the facility far from here?"

"No, Madame. Quarter of an hour by car."

"Can you take me there?"

It was the longest fifteen-minute drive Sam could remember. Marcelle, still buoyant from yesterday's glamorous circus party, was reliving the highlights and Sam nodded when needed, murmuring appropriate responses even as she struggled to suppress her turbulent emotions.

Relax, she told herself. It's not the end of the world if Cristiano takes Gabriela to the track. Gabriela would probably enjoy watching the action on the racetrack but even then, Sam felt deeply disapproving. Racetracks were no place for children, much less young children Gabby's age.

Marcelle walked Sam through the private entrance reserved for drivers and crew, escorted her down to the track and pointed out a white car as it zoomed by.

"There they are," Marcelle said. "That's an Italia Motors car, you can tell by the insignia, and the number—that's Monsieur's number."

Sam nodded distractedly, looking around for Gabby. "But where's Gabriela? Who's watching her?"

"Oh, Madame, not to worry. She's with Monsieur."

"With Cristiano?"

"*Oui*, Madame. In the car."

It might have only been five minutes before Cristiano pulled into the pit and opened the door, allowing Gabby to scamper out, but for Sam it was a lifetime.

Every possible thought went through her head, every possible emotion swept her, every possible scenario had played out.

Heart in her throat, Sam watched them approach. How could

he do it? How could he be so stupid? So selfish? How could he put Gabby in the car with him?

Gabby spotting Sam, shouted her name and waved. Cristiano smiled, let Gabby's hand go so she could race to Sam's side.

Shaking, Sam grabbed blindly for Gabriela, settled her arms around Gabby's neck and shoulders. "How could you do that?" Sam demanded once Cristiano was at her side. "How could you do something like that?"

Cristiano hesitated, his smile fading. "I just took her for a drive—"

"But not at 200 mph!"

"I wasn't going 200 mph. I wasn't even going over 100."

Sam's legs felt as though they were going to give out. "Where was she sitting?"

"In my lap."

"*Your* lap."

Gabby twisted away, looked up at Sam. "He was teaching me to drive."

Sam wanted to laugh, she felt nearly hysterical. "Oh, that's just marvelous. Gabby turns five yesterday so now it's time to teach her to drive?"

"It's not the first time, Sam," Gabby answered seriously. "I like driving."

"Not the first time?" Sam crouched down, looked Gabby in the eye. "What do you mean this isn't the first time?"

"It's not. I come here with Cristiano before school sometimes."

"*No.*"

"Sam," Cristiano said. "Let's not put her in the middle of this."

"Not put her in the middle? Cristiano, you've already put her in the middle! You've been sneaking her to the track—"

"There's been no sneaking. I don't sneak around. This is my life. This is what I do."

"But a *child!*" Sam couldn't believe it, couldn't accept it. "Cristiano, you've pushed it too far. You've behaved recklessly, thoughtlessly—"

"Marcelle," Cristiano shouted to the young woman where she stood by the wall. "Would you mind taking Gabby home for lunch?"

"No problem, Monsieur." Marcelle hurried toward them, swept Gabby into her arms and dashed away.

Sam waited for Marcelle and Gabby to disappear before continuing. "You can take risks with your life but you've no right to take risks with hers."

"I'm very careful with her, Sam. I don't drive fast when she's in the car, but driving, racing, it's part of her, Sam, part of who she is and who her father was—who her *brother* is."

"No more. You can't bring her here anymore. You can't take her in your car—"

"I've spent five years trying to get her back."

"Not very hard it seems. Where were you when she was born? Where were you when she was one?"

"I was in a hospital, Sam. I was hurt, and learning to walk again. And yes, it was a driving accident that burned me, and yes, it was a driving accident that killed my father, but I'm here now and I'm not going away."

"How can you say that? You could be killed in two weeks in Australia, and if not Australia, then Malaysia after!"

He was silent, his features hard, defiant. "You can't change me, Sam. You can accept me but you can't change me."

"Well, I can't accept you. I can't accept you'd risk everything—me, Gabby, your future—for a sport!"

"It's not a sport, it's my career."

"Your *career*."

"And just how strongly do you feel about this, Sam?" His voice had dropped, become ice-cold.

She felt the distance yawn between them, the distance greater now than it'd ever been.

Sam was too upset, too angry, too heartsick to even cry. It had all come down to this. The worries, the fears, the anxiety had been building in her since she discovered just what it was he did professionally, but it was about to explode out now. "I'm not…I can't…"

"Can't what?" he demanded, voice clipped.

"Do this."

"Do what? Live with me? Love me? Accept me? What?"

Her eyes burned. Her chest burned. She burned all the way through and she could only imagine the agony Cristiano felt when his body really was on fire. "All of the above."

CHAPTER THIRTEEN

CRISTIANO stared at her, hearing the words she said but unable to believe it. "Do you even know what you're saying, Sam?"

Paling, she nodded. "I know I can't live worrying about you every time you get behind the wheel of a car."

"Then don't worry. I've been driving since I was eleven. Won my first kart race at thirteen. Sam, I've made mistakes, some I have to live with forever, but I'm not reckless."

She didn't say anything for a long moment, just stared at him with those blue eyes, anxiously pushing loose hair back from her face. "Why hasn't Gabby ever told me you've brought her to the track? Gabby tells me everything. Why didn't she tell me that?"

That's when Cristiano knew they'd turned a corner, headed a direction that might take them places they hadn't ever wanted to go. "I asked her not to."

How quickly her stormy blue gaze turned cold. *"Why?"*

"Because I told her you were afraid of cars and it might scare you, and I didn't want to upset you."

"And telling a five-year-old to cover the truth—essentially *lie* to me—wouldn't upset me?"

He was angry, too. Angry and tired. He'd slept like crap last night, his gut in knots, heart heavy. He didn't want to fight. He hated fights. All he wanted today was to have things better. "I thought your fear was irrational," he said finally, wearily.

"Irrational?" Sam's jaw jutted furiously. "I've lost everyone

I've loved in car accidents, and you have the gall to say it's *irrational?*"

"I'm not your parents, and I'm not Charles—"

"Cristiano! Have you looked at your legs? Have you seen what racing has done to you? How can you think you've escaped unscathed?"

He laughed, and it was a brutal sound. "I'm well aware of the risk, and the price we pay. But I've accepted it and I deal with it, and if you want a life with me you have to deal with it, too."

Tears filled her eyes. "No. I don't have to deal with it. I won't deal with it. I love you, but I can't live like this. It'll destroy me—"

"Because you're letting it destroy you. Make a different choice—"

"Why don't *you* make a different choice? Why don't you compromise? Why should I be the one to have to change?"

"Because this is what I love to do more than anything else in the world."

And that just about said it all, she thought, holding her breath and looking at him.

He did love his cars and racing more than anything else. He loved the danger and the adrenaline. He loved competition. He loved to win.

But he had to also understand how she felt about him, how frightened she was of losing him. He had to know that life would be unbearable for her and for Gabby if something happened to him now.

She turned her head and looked at him, really looked at him for the first time in a long time, taking him in as if trying to remember. There was so much she loved about him, so much she loved in his face—the shape of his jaw, the quirk of his mouth, the lips that felt so right on hers…

"I'm sorry, Cristiano." She felt the tears well but she wouldn't let them fall, not today, not this time. She didn't understand this emotion, didn't understand what was making her feel so fierce, so wild, so volatile. Was it love? Hate? Was it something else?

She didn't know, and what she did know was that she craved peace. Peace for her heart, peace for her mind. Peace from the chaos rioting inside her. Love, hate, whatever it was—she didn't want it anymore. She just wanted relief. "I've lost my parents in a car accident, Charles in a car accident, and I'm not going to lose you, too. Not that way."

He made a rough, guttural sound in the back of his throat. "No, you'll just lose me another way."

"I *don't* want to lose you."

He gave her a long hard look. "Sam, I'm beginning to think you don't even know who I am."

"I know who you are."

"Then you know what I do."

"How can you love your work more than—"

"Don't even go there. You can't say that. I won't let you."

Maybe he didn't love his work more, but he did love the danger. He lived for the adrenaline rush. He was a risk-taker, a thrill-seeker, a man that thrived on pushing his limits over and over again.

He wanted to be great. Wanted to be famous. He wanted to make a name that equaled—if not eclipsed—his father's. But men became famous in one of two ways—they did something death defying, or they died. Either way it was dangerous. Either way, those who loved him would suffer. And Sam didn't want to suffer anymore. She didn't want to fear, or worry. She didn't want to go to bed alone, or wake up alone, and miss. She was so sick of missing.

Life had to get easier.

It had to get easier.

"I won't give up racing, Sam," he said quietly. "I won't give it up for you, won't give it up for anyone. If you care for me, you accept me for who I am…not for who you want me to be."

"Fine. Don't give up racing. But I'm not going to another funeral, and in your sport—profession—people die. Maybe not every race, but every year, and these aren't old men, Cristiano. They're young. They're twenty-four, twenty-seven, thirty, thirty-four, thirty-seven…they're fathers, brothers, husbands, lovers. They're men just like you."

"Sam, there's risk in everything."

She just shot him a long, disapproving glance. There was risk, and there was *risk*. He was a smart man. He had to know the difference.

"I'll take you back," he said.

She nodded woodenly. That was that then. She exhaled slowly as she walked with him to his car.

They rode in silence as he drove back to Cap Ferrat. As he pulled through the villa's wrought-iron gates, she glanced at him. His jaw was thick, hard, tight. In front of the villa, he shifted into park, but he didn't turn off the engine.

During the drive she'd stared out the window, not letting herself think, not letting herself feel, but now that they were here, she was afraid to get out of the car. Afraid of what would happen next. "You're not coming in?"

"No."

"What will you do?"

"Go back to Monte Carlo."

She swallowed the lump in her throat, rubbed her hands together, the friction keeping her distracted long enough to keep herself together. "When will we see you again?"

"We'll have to make arrangements regarding Gabby. I'm not going to lose her, or give her up. We'll just have to share her—"

"No."

"Yes." He made an impatient sound. "Sam, things are going to change. But we have to do what's best for Gabby."

"And what's best for Gabby?"

"Both of us. Which means, she'll spend part of each week with me, part with you. When I'm on the road, she'll stay with you, of course."

"We could always spend time with her together."

"I don't see us doing things together. I don't want to try to do things together, not if it's over." He looked at her, expression shuttered. "I tried, Sam, I really did."

She opened the car door, slid out. This was crazy, absolutely crazy. Only yesterday was Gabby's party. Only yesterday everything had been wonderful. Magical. Sam's eyes burned and she drew a quick breath, and then another. "I'll need a place to stay in Monte Carlo when I'm there with Gabby." Her voice broke, and she bit ruthlessly into her bottom lip. "Is Johann's villa still available?"

"That place is a dump."

"I don't mind."

"I do. I don't want Gabriela there."

Sam closed her eyes, wondering how on earth she'd explain any of this to Gabby. My God. It would break Gabby's heart. "What do we tell her, Cristiano?" Tears fell and she dashed them away with the back of her hand. "She loves you, she loves me, she loves the idea of us together."

Cristiano looked at her so long, his hazel-green gaze penetrating, it felt as though he'd pierced his heart. "So did I."

He revved the engine, reached for his sunglasses in the center console. "Stay here at the villa for now. Once I leave for Australia you and Gabby can have the penthouse. I'll get a place of my own."

"And what will I tell her—when you're off traveling for weeks at a time?"

He shrugged. "Tell her what most fathers who travel for business tell their kids. I'm working." He shifted gears and drove away.

Those first few days after Cristiano left were unreal—hard, hard, heartbreaking, lonely.

She couldn't sleep at night, she couldn't focus during the day. She wanted to call him, wanted to talk to him, wanted more than anything to hear his voice, to have him talk to her, miss her, love her.

But he didn't call and he didn't reach out to her and it seemed—as difficult as it was to believe—that he really intended for it to be over.

The weeks passed, slowly, very slowly until it had been a month since Cristiano left and by the end of March Sam felt like the walking dead.

The villa on Cap Ferrat was still gorgeous, the gardens still perfectly manicured, the views as breathtaking, but Sam couldn't find pleasure in it anymore. In bed at night, she tossed and turned. She'd try to sleep but couldn't stop thinking long enough to let sleep come. Some nights she just gave up pretending sleep would come and then she'd leave bed to go out on her balcony. Sitting there, wrapped in a blanket, she'd look at the stars and listen to the ocean and fight tears.

It was crazy, absolutely crazy. Charles and her parents were killed in car accidents and she was so scared of cars, and scared to drive, she hadn't driven a car in years. She didn't even like being a passenger in other people's cars. And yet who did she fall in love with?

A Grand Prix driver.

Curled in the chair on her balcony, Sam dragged the blanket more tightly around her shoulders, burying her chin in her blanket-covered knees.

She couldn't believe she'd given Cristiano an ultimatum.

Worse, she couldn't believe he'd accepted it.

What a fool she was. Not just for giving him an ultimatum, but for missing him as much as she did. Because even now, in late March, she found herself still waiting for his Italia Motors sports car to appear, or the phone to ring and discover it was Cristiano on the line.

But he didn't call her. He didn't communicate directly with her. He sent messages, terse e-mails, conversations and discussions through Marcelle who had somehow—and this was perhaps one of the hardest things to swallow—become Gabriela's new nanny.

It was Marcelle who chauffeured Gabby to the parties and playdates that began streaming in once people knew that darling little Gabriela, was actually Gabriela *Bartolo*.

It was Marcelle who updated Cristiano on Gabby's progress in school and extracurricular activities.

It was Marcelle who advised Cristiano when Gabby seemed tired or a little under the weather.

Sam might resent Cristiano for cutting her so completely out of his life, but she did admire his devotion to Gabby. He called her daily, no matter where he was on the road, as attentive to her now, as when they all lived together. Three weeks ago he was phoning Gabby from Australia, ten days ago it was Malaysia, and now Bahrain.

He was doing well on the road right now, too. He took first in Australia, third in Malaysia and first again in Bahrain. Sam might have a broken heart, but Cristiano was on a roll.

Less than a week later, Cristiano was back in town. She hoped she'd see him, maybe have a chance to talk to him when he collected Gabby for the weekend, but she didn't even know he'd been at the villa until Sam saw Marcelle walking Gabby out to the car.

Cristiano didn't linger. He took off once Gabriela was buckled up and Sam watched the two people she loved best in the world disappear for a weekend together.

She was truly on the outs. And it hurt. And the hurt didn't get better, it was just getting worse.

I'm so lonely, Sam thought. I'm lonely and lost and this is how I felt when Charles died, only no one's died. Cristiano was very much alive—traveling and working and racing and being interviewed on television.

How ironic that she, who hated cars and racing, now watched everything she could about the Grand Prix.

No, he wasn't dead. He was just moving on with his life, and excluding her from it.

Sam tried to distract herself that weekend while Gabby was with Cristiano. She took walks down to the water, walks into the village, walks through the Rothschild garden and museum.

But the walking didn't stop her from thinking, and it didn't stop her from feeling.

Sam loved Cristiano like mad. She missed him so much she felt shattered inside. It wasn't one thing she missed, it was everything.

She missed the way they talked late at night with the TV turned down low.

She missed the way they used to smile at each other over Gabby's head when she said something particularly funny.

She missed his sexy voice, his even deeper, sexy laugh.

She missed the way he touched her low on her back.

She missed the way when he hugged her, he'd bring her so close and her insides would flip—eager, responsive, excited.

She missed making love—God, she missed making love.

She missed the life she'd had with him...even if it had been brief.

Shaking her head, she tried to chase away the pictures filling her head, pictures of him, and her, and them together, pictures that were tormenting her heart.

If only she hadn't lost so many people in her life. If only she were a different person altogether.

Sam drew a deep breath, battling for her famous British stiff upper lip, the one Cristiano had teased her about, but if only he knew, the lip wasn't very stiff.

The lip, as a matter of fact, was trembling.

Sunday afternoon finally arrived. Gabby should return by dinner. To pass time Sam tidied Gabby's room, sorted clothes, reorganized toys and then with nothing left to do, headed outside to visit the garden.

Restlessly she wandered around the garden, through flower beds and then past the fountains to the pool.

Taking a seat on one of the chaise lounges at the pool, Sam pulled her knees up against her, propped her chin on her hand and gazed out at the ocean. The sea was still so beautiful here, layers of cobalt-blue and azure-green. She didn't think she'd ever get tired of looking at the water, and as long as she just concentrated on the water, on the tide and the breaking surf, she'd be okay. But the moment she lost focus, the moment she let herself think about her, Gabby, Cristiano—she just lost it.

She loved Cristiano.

And that's all it took for her eyes to fill with tears, and her mind to spin off in futile directions.

She loved Cristiano but he wanted different things than she did. He wanted glory and she just wanted security. Family. *Peace.*

Closing her eyes, she wouldn't let herself cry. She'd cried far too much this past month. Cristiano's not dead, she told herself, he's just away.

And he'll come back. He will. He has to.

Next time she opened her eyes the sun was lower in the sky and a light blanket covered her shoulders. Blinking, disoriented, Sam shifted, stared up straight into Cristiano's shadowed face.

Cristiano? Sam sat up swiftly, knocking the blanket off her in her haste. "What are you doing here?"

"Brought Gabby home."

"What time is it?"

"Almost six."

"Six?" She put a hand to her head, still dizzy from sitting up so quickly. "That long?"

"You've been asleep since I got here, and we've been back a couple of hours."

Sam stood, busied herself folding the blanket. "Where's Gabby?"

"Playing in her room."

This was so strange, she thought, surreal. She hadn't seen or talked to Cristiano in weeks and weeks and she'd done nothing but miss him and now here he was and they were having a conversation as if it were the most normal thing in the world.

The fact that they could have a normal conversation made it that much worse.

There was no reason for them not to be together. There was no reason...

Other than the fact that she feared losing him in a violent accident and he refused to acknowledge how difficult, or heartbreaking, such a loss would be for her and Gabby.

"Congratulations on the win in Bahrain," she said now, holding the blanket against her as she faced him. She was so full of conflicting emotions, emotions that hadn't dulled in the weeks since they said goodbye.

Some people just felt right, she thought.

Some people just made sense.

And except for this crazy, dangerous, reckless career of Cristiano's….he made perfect sense to her.

"Thanks," he answered, hesitating. "How is everything?"

Her gaze searched his. God, she'd missed him, missed that face, the deep grooves near his mouth, the fine creases at his eyes, the dark hair, the mouth…kissing that mouth.

Horrible, she wanted to tell him. *Terrible. I hate life without you, I hate that you've moved on so quickly, moved on so completely without me.* "Fine."

Her voice wobbled and she forced herself to smile to keep the sadness from showing in her face.

She adored Gabby, loved being with Gabriela, but she wanted more than to be just maternal. She wanted the rest of being a woman—the love, the passion, the skin, the sex. To be a lover, not just a mother.

"You're well?" he persisted.

She nodded, not trusting herself to speak this time.

His hazel-green eyes narrowed as he studied her, expression shuttered, giving nothing away. "You look tired."

She started for the house and he fell in beside her. "I don't sleep as well," she said carefully. "But it's probably just all the changes."

His mouth tugged grimly. "Chef Sacchi said you don't eat anything he makes anymore."

"I eat."

His gaze was critical as it swept over her. "No, it doesn't look like you do. You've lost weight, and you were already thin to start with. I can't have you starving yourself. It's not a good example for Gabby—"

"I'm *not* starving myself. Okay?" And if he could eat, great, but how was she supposed to get food down when it felt as if her heart was always in her mouth?

They'd reached the villa's veranda and Cristiano stopped walking. He looked up at the house where the late-afternoon sun reflected red-gold off the second story windowpanes. "I wanted to talk to you about Gabby's summer plans." He paused before continuing. "Gabby's school holidays are coming up and I'd like her to go to the United States Grand Prix with me in June."

United States in June? Gabby go halfway around the world without her? Sam balled her hands. "For how long?"

"Two to three weeks."

Eternity. Sam exhaled slowly. "That's an awfully long trip."

"It'd be a great opportunity for her to see more of the world, and you know Gabby, she'd love it. She's so curious, just a great little traveler."

"You'll be competing?"

"Yes."

She frowned. "So how will you…"

"Marcelle will be there."

"Marcelle's going to the United States with you?"

"Sam, Gabby's only five. She needs someone to look after—" He broke off and then shook his head. "I'm sorry. But of course you know that. You've spent more time with her than anyone. You used to be her nanny."

Used to be her nanny. Well, that was putting her in her place. No wives or mothers, no best friends or lovers. Just the nanny. Back to the hired help.

Sam would have laughed if it weren't so bloody painful. Because of course he was right. She was the nanny and she'd served her purpose.

But that didn't mean Sam didn't wish she could be Marcelle because Sam wanted to be going to America in June. She wanted to go to the United States Grand Prix. She wanted to be at the track and watch Cristiano race.

"Tell Gabby goodbye for me," he said pulling out his car keys. "She'd wanted me to stay for dinner but it's not a very good idea."

"You're welcome to stay—"

"No. It'll just get her hopes up, make her want something that's not going to happen."

"What's not going to happen?"

"This." He gestured at the villa, at her, at the twilight. "What was. What we were."

So it was done, all over, there'd be no going back, and no second chances.

Silently they walked around the side of the house to the driveway where his Italia Motors sports car waited. He opened the driver's side door but didn't climb in. Instead he folded his arms across his chest and stared down at her, hazel eyes dark, unreadable. "I hope someday you'll find whatever it is you're looking for."

Her eyes burned and she blinked. "You might not believe it, but I was looking for you."

"You were looking for a safe, sanitized version of me, but not me, because if it were me, we'd still be together."

Sam stared up at him, seeing the face she loved and the man she admired and despite his new stiffness she could still feel the man somewhere in there. "Why can't you see that you're so valuable, a woman wouldn't want to lose you? Why can't you see that it's not selfishness, but love?"

"Then it's a very controlling love, and I don't want to be controlled. I want to be accepted. Big difference." He slid behind the steering wheel, closed the door. "And you're not the only one afraid, Sam. Love is scary—and risky—for everyone.

"*Bella,* you have to live while you're alive."

CHAPTER FOURTEEN

THE phone rang and Sam leaned across her bed to answer it. Probably yet another call for Gabby from one of her friends. With her famous father winning two of his last three big races, Gabriela Grace Bartolo had become the most popular little girl in the Côte d'Azur.

"Hello?" Sam answered, punching the mute button on the TV remote control.

"Sam."

Cristiano. They hadn't spoken in weeks, not since that day he'd dropped Gabby off before the San Marino Grand Prix. She swallowed, her hand gripping the phone tightly. "Hi."

"Do you have a minute?" His voice was hard, clipped, impersonal. She could have been anyone.

And maybe that was the punishment. She was just anyone.

"Yes. Gabby's already in bed asleep."

Silence stretched across the line, a silence where Sam wanted words, where she wanted warmth, and more than anything, she wanted comfort.

Tell me it's going to be okay.

Tell me you still love me.

Tell me we can make this work, because I want this to work.

"Do you have a lawyer?" he asked.

"A lawyer?"

"To represent you."

Sam drew her knees up against her, wrapped an arm around her knees, hugging them close. "Do I need one?"

"You should. It's smart. That way you're protected. You'll have someone looking after your best interest."

And I thought that would be you. I thought you'd be looking after my best interests for years to come.

"If you need some names—"

"You're going to help me get a lawyer for our divorce?"

He hesitated for a fraction of a second, and his silence was even colder than his voice. "I don't want you to think I'm taking advantage of you."

A huge lump filled her throat making it almost impossible to breathe right much less speak. "You've never taken advantage of me before. I wouldn't think you'd take advantage of me now."

"When it's over, Sam, it's over."

"I don't understand what that's supposed to mean."

"It means if you want something, get it now."

Get it? Get what? "And just what do you think I want to get?"

"Your piece of the pie."

My God, the expression sounded absolutely horrible coming from his mouth, especially in light of what they were discussing now. "I have never cared about your money! You know that, Cristiano."

"You deserve some security, Sam, get it. I'll see that my assistant forwards the referrals. They're all names of people you could trust—"

"Cristiano," she spoke urgently, unable to keep from interrupting, panic and fear, hurt and disbelief tumbling one over the other inside her. Their first meeting had come from nowhere, sudden, explosive. She couldn't bear to think their end would be the same. "Does it have to be this way?"

More silence stretched across the phone line. "I promised I would always look after you, the way you looked after Gabriela."

Sam couldn't completely stifle her cry despite covering her

nose and mouth so he couldn't hear. The tears were falling, great tears that couldn't be stopped. "I'm sorry." Her voice shook and she wiped at her nose. "Cristiano, I'm so sorry."

"I am, too." Yet his voice was as dead as dead could be. "You'll keep the villa, and the Monte Carlo penthouse. Twenty thousand a month maintenance. Twenty thousand child support. Does that sound fair?"

No, she wanted to cry. No, it sounds lousy. I don't want your money. I don't want your home. I just want you.

"You'll receive the first set of papers by the end of the week. Have your lawyer read them over and then get back to me." He paused again, and the silence stretched. "Any questions?"

"No."

"Sam, I don't want to drag this out. It'll only hurt and confuse Gabriela."

Fist pressed to her heart, she told herself to just get through the rest of the call. Just make it to the end and then get off the phone. You can cry all you want then. "I understand."

"I don't want this in the news, either—"

"I'd never go to them."

"Good. I guess that's it then."

He must have said goodbye because suddenly there was a click and he was no longer there, no longer on the line.

Slowly Sam put the phone back down and even more slowly she stretched out on her stomach on the bed, burying her face in the crook of her arm.

She used to panic, thinking she couldn't bear to lose him, couldn't contemplate life without him.

And she had lost him.

But he wasn't dying. He was divorcing her.

Which in some ways was so much worse because it's not as if they didn't have other options, it's not as if they couldn't have found a way to work through their differences. Especially as there had been so much good between them, so much good worth saving.

So much worth fighting for.

He hadn't fought for it—them—their relationship. But then, neither had she.

It was the strangest thing—her head snapped back, eyes opening, jaw dropping slightly before she snapped her mouth closed and sat up and threw her legs on the side of the bed.

She hadn't fought for them at all.

Why not?

Sam left the bed, paced her room and going to the balcony pushed the doors open to step out into the night.

She hadn't fought. It made no sense. Sam adored Gabby because she was feisty, spirited, courageous. Sam had admired Cristiano for his strength, not just the physical strength, but the mental strength necessary to come back from his devastating accident. Both Gabby and Cristiano were tough. Brave. Fighters. And Sam wanted that. She wanted their courage. Their strength. Their fight.

If Charles could teach her kindness and compassion, then Cristiano and Gabriela could teach her to stand fast. To be brave. To charge the battle.

Charge the battle.

Sam leaned on the balcony railing, and staring out at the dark sea and night Sam thought of all the challenges she'd faced in her own life, and maybe she hadn't dealt with them easily, or gracefully, but she'd moved forward. She'd learned. Changed. Adapted.

She could do it again.

She could learn to be strong. To face her fears. To acknowledge risk.

She closed her eyes, pictured herself a warrior, sword in hand, armor on, standing fast before dragons and men.

Maybe not before dragons, but certainly before men.

She *could* be brave. She could be strong. She could face danger head on.

Now if she could only find some really good armor because she was going to need it. Bad.

* * *

Four days later, Sam sat in Marcelle's car outside the *Automobile Monegasque,* the track Bartolo Driving School used for its European school.

"Marcelle, you can't tell anyone," Sam said, knotting and un-knotting her hands. "No one can know in case I fail miserably."

"You won't fail, and I won't tell." Marcelle leaned on the steering wheel and smiled encouragingly. Marcelle was dropping her off for the first day of a weeklong course with the objective of preparing drivers for road racing. "Just have fun, Madame."

Sam shot Marcelle a dubious glance before climbing out of the car. Marcelle tooted her horn and drove away leaving Sam alone in the parking lot.

This was it, Sam thought, facing the low building fronting the racetrack. She was going to school. Today was a refresher course called High Performance Driving, tomorrow was Intro to Racing, and by week's end she'd be clocking it on the track in the open-wheel Formula 1 cars.

This was going to be the worst week of her life.

She was nervous that first day, so nervous she threw up twice in the morning and once in the afternoon, but she made it through the day.

Tuesday was as rough.

Wednesday not quite so bad. She almost liked the Corvette C5 they had her driving.

Thursday she was introduced to the pit. She didn't like the pit—it was noisy, frenetic, but she got a lesson in spark plugs, engines, and changing tires anyway.

Friday was race day and Sam was throwing up again. As she approached the low sleek F1 car, Sam tugged the zipper on her jumpsuit down instead of up. She was going to throw up again. And making a mad dash to the bathroom, she got sick, washed her face, and stared at herself in the mirror.

All you have to do is drive, she told herself. You don't have to drive fast. You don't have to be brilliant. All you have to do is drive around the track. You'll be safe.

Coming out of the bathroom she tugged the zipper on her protective jumpsuit up, slicked her hair into a ponytail and met Rodney, her instructor, at her car.

Rodney, a young Scottish driver with an impressive track record, grinned at her as he saw her approach. "You're looking like a right happy lass."

"Don't try to humor me today, Rodney."

He clapped her on the back. "I'm going to be in a car out there with you. Follow me on the track, stay close, hug the turns and, girl, have some fun."

This would not be fun but she was going to do it anyway. She was going to look fear in the face and prove once and for all that fear didn't master her—she was going to master it.

In the pit, Cristiano glanced at his watch yet again. It was twenty past noon and the track should be cleared. This was his practice time, the time when he tested the different cars, checked them to see how they were running.

He leaned against the side of his car, helmet on his lap. "Who's still out there?" he asked one of his pit crew.

The mechanic nodded at the yellow car screaming past. "Rodney."

"He's giving a lesson now?" Cristiano asked as a blue F1 student car chased behind.

"He should be done soon."

"He should have been done twenty minutes ago." Cristiano stood, turned to his team. "Somebody bring out the flag. Let's get him out of here. I've got work to do."

"Right, boss," the mechanic answered and one of the others drew out a red flag and waved it back and forth.

Cristiano zipped up his practice suit and waited for Rodney to exit the track. Instead Rodney pulled up next to Cristiano in the pit, Rodney's student pulling up behind him.

Climbing out of his yellow car Rodney waved cheerfully to Cristiano. "Hey, how's it going?"

Cristiano's bad mood was getting worse. "What are you still doing on the track? Lessons are mornings only."

Rodney shrugged, dropped his helmet in his car. "Couldn't

help it, boss. She needed a little extra time. Nerves and all. She had a bad case of them but I think we worked most the kinks out today. How'd she look?"

Cristiano swore softly beneath his breath. He was not in the mood for games. "Fine. Why?"

Rodney opened the door to his student's car and bending over, unbuckled the chin strap and gestured for her to remove her helmet. "Come meet the boss."

Cristiano didn't hear anything once he saw the helmet come off and a long blond ponytail tumble out.

"Santo Cielo!" Cristiano strode furiously toward the blue car where Sam still sat strapped into the seat. "What the hell is going on?"

Rodney lifted his hands in an innocent shrug. "I was just teaching her to drive. She paid for the lessons. All week. She's been here every day, all day."

"Thanks, Rodney," Cristiano growled. "I've got it from here."

"You're the boss," Rodney answered with a jaunty whistle as he strolled away.

Sam clutched the steering wheel as she watched Cristiano walk toward her.

He was livid. He'd always had a big jaw but it was a lot bigger right now.

Cristiano leaned on the side of the car, towering over her. And then he swore. Neither softly, nor gently. "What the hell are you doing?"

Sam wasn't sure where to look because she didn't want to look into his face, not when he looked so spitting mad. "Learning to drive."

"A Formula 1 car?"

"I've been practicing in other cars, too."

He was dead silent. He didn't laugh, or crack a smile, not even a little bit. "These are difficult to drive, Sam. They're not the kind of cars you just climb in."

"Tell me about it! I've never in my life had to study, or work this hard."

He pushed up off the car. "Sam, this is dangerous, and Rodney's a good driver, a decent instructor, but he—" Cristiano broke off, shook his head "—he, what were you thinking taking lessons from *him?*"

"*Him?* What do you mean by him? Rodney Sterling is one of your top instructors."

"I would have never trusted him with you. I wouldn't have let him take you on the track, not even once. Never. Not in a thousand years—"

He broke off as she started laughing. He had to be joking, she thought, had to be. But his expression didn't soften. It just grew stonier. "Cristiano." She tried to keep from smiling. He looked so grim right now, so autocratic. "He was a great teacher. And I learned a lot. Look. I'm driving. I'm driving an F1 car. And I'm still here. I'm alive."

"Something could have happened. You could have lost control—"

"I took the class you designed. I learned from the best. There were indoor lessons, track lessons. I wore a jumpsuit. A seat belt. I was completely safe."

"No one is ever completely safe."

"Now look who's talking!"

"I just know the dangers, Sam."

She shook her head, unable to believe how he'd changed his tune. When he was behind the wheel taking risks, it was fine. But when it was her, it wasn't? "You don't trust me."

"It's not a matter of trust."

"Yes, it is. You think you can take crazy risks and survive them. And I can't even take small risks—"

"I don't want you to take risks."

"Life is full of risks, Cristiano! You and I both know that, but weren't you also the one that taught me to seize life. Live it. Charge the battle?"

He looked at her, carefully, expression intense, agonized, revealing a depth of emotion he let few see. "You hate cars, *bella*."

"I know." She swallowed, and bit her lip, suddenly shy. "But

I love you more than I hate cars, so I decided I'd try to face my fears and take some risks."

He caught her chin in his hand, and leaning into the car, kissed her. "These were some significant fears, *bella*. Ones that made you leave me."

"I don't want to lose you, Cristiano. I don't want to let you go…not without a fight." Tears filled her eyes and she reached up, touched his face lightly, lovingly, wonderingly. For three months she'd missed him and missed him and the missing would never have gone away. "Please give me a chance to fight for you." Her fingers brushed his cheekbone and then down to his mouth. "Please give me a chance—"

"*Bella*, I think you've got it."

"You have to know I love you. I love you and Gabby and the two of you are my family. And I'd do anything for my family, anything to keep my family together. Please—"

"Done."

"Done?"

He hauled her out of the car, pulled her against him, his arms wrapping securely around her. "We're yours. *I'm* yours."

"You don't believe in love—"

"I lied. I need yours."

That settled it. Sealed the deal. She'd loved him ever since he'd trudged through the snow, building a snowman without gloves with Gabriela in Cheshire, but this, this is what she needed to hear. Selfish as it was, she needed to know he loved her for her. That he wanted her, Samantha Anne Hill, for no other reason than he loved her.

"You have it," she said, leaning against him, wrapping her arms around his lean torso and kissing him. "For the next fifty years. At home, in your corporate office, on the jet, at the track, in the pit—"

"Ahem." He coughed, cleared his throat. "Maybe home and the jet's enough. I don't think I could concentrate enough to win a race if you're down on the track, or in the pit."

"What about the corporate office?"

"What about the nursery at home?" He teased, hazel-green eyes glinting. "Maybe you need a baby to keep you busy since Gabby is getting so independent."

She blushed, smiled, cheeks hot. "I could get used to the idea of a baby."

"And maybe in a year or so with a baby in the house, I won't need to travel so much."

"You don't mean that."

"But I do. I'm having a great year—I've never done better—but at the end of the season I'm going to take some time off, concentrate on my driving schools for a while."

"Why?"

He caressed her warm cheek with his thumb. "I'm thinking about retiring."

Sam pushed away from his chest, looked up at him. "Retire? Now? Just when I'm getting into the racing scene?"

Cristiano laughed and pulled her close again, his lips covering hers, taking her breath in a long, slow head-spinning kiss. "Exactly what I was afraid of." He kissed her once more. "Before I know it you'll be camping out at the track trying to get all the drivers' autographs."

She grinned. "I don't think that's going to happen. Not if I've got you at home." She leaned toward him and kissed him, and as she kissed him the laughter faded, replaced by fierce determination, the kind of determination that comes from knowing what matters most in the world. "Just come home and make us a real family again. That's all I want—all I'll ever want. Not things. Not fame. Not fortune. Just family."

"*Our* family."

"Exactly."

HARLEQUIN *Presents*

**Don't miss the latest story
by favorite Presents author**

Lynne Graham

THE SHEIKH'S
INNOCENT BRIDE

#2511 January 2006

Feel warm winds blowing through your hair and the
hot desert sun on your skin as you are transported to
Prince Shahir's exotic kingdom…. As the temperature
rises, enjoy the story of the sexy sheikh and his lowly
cleaner Kirsten Ross. She was innocent—now she's
pregnant with a royal baby!

www.eHarlequin.com

HPTSIB

If you enjoyed what you just read,
then we've got an offer you can't resist!

Take 2 bestselling
love stories FREE!

Plus get a FREE surprise gift!

Clip this page and mail it to Harlequin Reader Service®

IN U.S.A.	IN CANADA
3010 Walden Ave.	P.O. Box 609
P.O. Box 1867	Fort Erie, Ontario
Buffalo, N.Y. 14240-1867	L2A 5X3

YES! Please send me 2 free Harlequin Presents® novels and my free surprise gift. After receiving them, if I don't wish to receive anymore, I can return the shipping statement marked cancel. If I don't cancel, I will receive 6 brand-new novels every month, before they're available in stores! In the U.S.A., bill me at the bargain price of $3.80 plus 25¢ shipping & handling per book and applicable sales tax, if any*. In Canada, bill me at the bargain price of $4.47 plus 25¢ shipping & handling per book and applicable taxes**. That's the complete price and a savings of at least 10% off the cover prices—what a great deal! I understand that accepting the 2 free books and gift places me under no obligation ever to buy any books. I can always return a shipment and cancel at any time. Even if I never buy another book from Harlequin, the 2 free books and gift are mine to keep forever.

106 HDN DZ7Y
306 HDN DZ7Z

Name   (PLEASE PRINT)

Address   Apt.#

City   State/Prov.   Zip/Postal Code

Not valid to current Harlequin Presents® subscribers.

Want to try two free books from another series?
Call 1-800-873-8635 or visit www.morefreebooks.com.

* Terms and prices subject to change without notice. Sales tax applicable in N.Y.
** Canadian residents will be charged applicable provincial taxes and GST.
   All orders subject to approval. Offer limited to one per household.
   ® are registered trademarks owned and used by the trademark owner and or its licensee.

PRES04R   ©2004 Harlequin Enterprises Limited